A novel by

Manuel P. Godoy Jr.

In collaboration with PHNX

Published by

Published by Black Sands Entertainment

www.blacksandsentertainment.com

mgodoy@blacksandsentertainment.com

Cover design by David Lenormand

Copyright © 2017 by Manuel P. Godoy Jr.
All rights reserved.
ISBN: 0999473417
ISBN 13: 9780999473412

This story was written for my Kickstarter backers and patrons. Without your support, we would never be able to create this much content for everyone.

This book is dedicated to Geiszel Godoy, my wife of eight years; Mori, my son; and Valencia, my daughter. Without you guys, I would be quite an uninteresting and incomplete man.

CONTENTS

1 THE ANCIENTS

It was around 15,000 BC when a faraway alien race grew interested in this strange planet called Earth. While the dominant species of Earth were primitive, the diversity of life inhabiting this biosphere, even among humanoids, proved too enticing for the extraterrestrials to ignore.

On their home world of Nibiru, locked in a wide elliptical orbit about the Sirius star system, there were only three distinct species. Each had been forced to evolve in order to survive the harsh cycles of the tidal-locked planet.

There were three stars within the Sirius system. Sirius A and Sirius B were binary and rotated around each other. The third, Sirius C, was a rogue star and completed its orbit once every 189 years. With each passage through Nibiru's path, the star would heat up the atmosphere to a boiling, uninhabitable 914 degrees Fahrenheit, incinerating every living creature on the planet's surface.

Nibiru was a doomed world, one of unending fire and unyielding frost—a perpetual cycle resulting in calamitous surface conditions that slowly formed after every pass and lasted for over a century.

The species had a rapid evolution, one born of necessity. On Nibiru, biological flesh was nothing more than a weakness, an evolutionary liability. As a means to combat such extreme planetary conditions, the Ancients who inhabited the planet evolved to be entirely elemental. But it was this evolution that ultimately led to their doom.

In time, their civilization developed the mental capacity to understand, and soon master, space travel. In a frantic means for continued survival, they made various attempts to settle numerous planets similar to their own—Ewatne, Opheliae, Hydrux, and others.

But their elemental bodies proved unable to adapt to these planets' native environments. Despite their extensive use of advanced technology, with each attempt, the colonizers would last no more than months on the alien terrain.

Faced with the impending certainty that the rogue star would one day soon traverse close enough to annihilate their world, the inhabitants of Nibiru collectively agreed to awaken an ancient deity—one who had slept for tens of thousands of years.

Nun, the Creator.

Many rumors abounded as to what transpired in those final days, and the truth had a strange way of morphing over the course of 8,611 light years. But whatever the impetus, Nun accepted the request of Nibiru's inhabitants.

It was with a grave sense of import that he bid the planet farewell and fired up his ancient ship, which had remained entombed miles below the Nibirun crust, and headed to Earth to begin again.

To endure the thousands of years it would take to travel such a distance, Nun placed himself in stasis, resuming his slumber.

He reached his destination, a tiny blue marble adrift in a sea of nothingness, during the fourth millennium BC. The exact location of his arrival was unknown, but it was thought to be somewhere within the cradle of life—that vast expanse somewhere between Africa and the Middle East.

Nun's ship was unlike any of the technology known even today. It was considered a Genesis-class ship, one imbued with the power to generate alterations within the very fabric of reality.

Upon impact, the ship triggered a tear in reality, suspending the craft within planet Earth but not quite *on* Earth itself.

The force of the crash caused the ship to burrow deep into the terrain, forming a vast crater that cradled the massive ship, sending its rear jutting high enough to rival the surrounding mountain peaks.

Nun awoke to the sound of the ship powering down and set about exploring the landscape of this new planet.

After he exited, he began to assess the damaged ship. The front was destroyed beyond repair. The rear—suspended from the crater. Waters used in the propulsion system began to seep out of the hull. Thick and almost gelatinous, those waters slowly oozed from the ship, forming the massive great lake, the Waters of Nun, in the surrounding crater. The waters swarmed the ship in a calm counterclockwise vortex that churned of its own volition.

Nun made his way to the highest cliff overlooking the landscape. It was from there that he assessed the situation. The surrounding terrain was wild but habitable. Its lush foliage and abundant waters differed vastly from the harsh, rocky terrain of Nibiru. He saw a mixture of jungles, mountains, and desert. It was almost incomprehensible, the diversity of this new land. Nun took it all in and nodded to himself. This would be the place.

Engulfing the entire landmass and faintly visible in the distance stood a large wall of black flames. Nun called this place the Rift, a void protected from the outside world—a sanctuary that protected the outside world from all contained within.

Nun's first task was to create his Black Temple, a

laboratory of sorts on the eastern side of the Rift. He decided upon osmium and iridium, elements that, while rare on Earth, were plentiful within the core of his ship.

Like a mad scientist, he toiled day and night inside the hulking pyramidal mass as he pondered how to replicate the Ancients in this new biome.

Using the elements of Earth, the mysterious crystals he'd gathered from Nibiru, and the waters from his ship to experiment with in his facility, Nun soon accomplished his task. The three races of Nibiru were replicated with modifications that enabled them to thrive in Earth's biosphere.

The first race called themselves Titans. Massive in size, they possessed an unusual affinity to the elements. But their appearance more often resembled monstrous creatures than men.

The second race called themselves Deva, and they were exceptional warriors. The Deva created superior technology and weaponry that advanced their destructive purpose, but inner conflict and growing animosity began to corrupt their kin.

Lastly were the Anunnaki, who remained focused on the advancement of human culture, unlike the others. Possessing incredible control over energy conversion, the Anunnaki were able to harness these powers to become great developers of architecture and power arrays.

Still, hundreds of years would pass before the Ancients were allowed to leave the Rift. In the interim, they trained under the watchful eye of Nun. Through his tutelage and the use of his omniscience, these first earthly creations learned of the outside world.

Each race was entrusted with one final goal: once they

acquired the necessary resources, they would aid their ancient predecessors on their home world—if they still existed.

When the time had come, Nun warned his creations that upon their exiting the Rift, they would never be able to return, for the black flames of the Rift would destroy all outside contamination and would disintegrate their being should they ever dare.

Accepting this fate, each race departed one by one to explore and eventually help build a greater society in the outside world.

It was predetermined that Nun could not venture forth with them. As an ancient being, he could only exist on the edge of reality.

Once the totality of his creation departed the Rift, Nun settled himself deep within his laboratory and resumed stasis.

That was one-thousand years ago. Nun was still in slumber but the black flames of the Rift grew restless. What does this disturbance mean, and what is Nun to do?

2 GOD KILLERS

A disturbance in the Rift—something has dared to enter the void. The disturbance is detected by the Black Temple. The alien crystals suspended throughout the structure tingle an alarm of warming. They awaken Nun from a slumber that, while lengthy in mortal years, has been a mere blip in the time span of Nun's everlasting existence.

He rises, still in a daze. As he studies the crystals that tremble around him, he struggles to remember the current year.

How could something survive entry into the Rift?

Regaining his composure, his massive body moves with a persistent stride as he makes his way outside to track the disturbance stemming from somewhere along the eastern flats.

He reaches the breach, a literal tear within the boundary that separates the Rift from the outside world.

Impossible!

He studies the ground beneath him and notices black flames scattered, their remnants leading toward the mountainous peaks in the northwest quadrant of the Rift.

He follows the path for miles, his mind pondering just who or what was powerful enough to breach his sacred domain.

He takes his time, keeping his senses alert until he sees movement up ahead, and squints in time to make out the intruder ever so slowly creeping away.

Enraged, Nun demands, "Who forces themselves into the Rift, forsaking life and disturbing my slumber?"

A cry of agony bellows from the trail. The being turns to

Nun with a strong green light emanating from its chest. Nun recognizes the aura. "Gaia?" he questions.

It is Gaia, the queen of the Titan bloodlines—master of nature itself.

Nun is horrified as he takes in her charred figure. *The consequences of breaching the Rift.* He shakes his head in sorrow, knowing that she is to die.

Drawing closer, he stops in his tracks once he glimpses the black flames eating away at her jade body. Once beautiful and luminescent, it now disintegrates slowly, as if being consumed by acid. Smoke fizzles atop skin that bubbles and boils. It's a grotesque sight with an equally rank odor that quickens the acids within the stomach.

"Gaia! Have you lost your mind?" Nun exclaims.

He's always shared a certain closeness with Gaia. Indeed, she was one of the few Ancients who believed in the traditions of the old world and the sanctity of life. Her purity was to be admired, for even Nun lacked the compassion she showed others.

"Why do you return?" Nun asks in disbelief.

"Father," Gaia struggles to say, "I come to you knowing that death will take me, to plead for your help."

Nun takes cautious steps toward Gaia as the black flames kindle on her limbs.

Nun reminds her, "The taint of the outside world cannot survive the flames of the Rift. They will purify you."

A tear falls from Gaia's eye as she drops to her crumbling knees that can no longer support her weight.

She gathers her composure before speaking. "I understand…that I will die. However, my purpose is of much more importance than my life. Allow me to explain before my body fades."

Nun gestures with a nod as he stands tall above her.

She continues, "My husband, Uranus, was looked upon by the humans as a god when we departed the Rift. We moved northwest to a mountainous land where humanity had taken root."

She coughs violently, causing the glow of her jade core to flicker. "Uranus looked down upon the humans and thought of them as nothing more than entertainment for him and his kin. He kept the secrets taught to us by you, but in his arrogance, he sought to recreate remnants of our home world here."

Clearly disturbed, Nun beckons her to continue. Gaia takes a moment, struggling to breathe before resuming. "Me and my family terraformed the land the humans call Greece into a preserve of ancient creatures. Over the years, I had given birth to children and expected that they would fix what their father had done. What I did not expect was the way Uranus would react to having children. A creeping paranoia began to take over his mind. His obsession with power was sickening, and worse yet was his belief that he was *losing* power. He, who had created all sorts of monstrosities, razed cities, and enslaved millions. How could he be losing his power?"

"That is because of the directive," Nun interjects.

"Directive?"

"Exterminating humans is unacceptable to the mission I gave you," Nun explains. "It is hard-coded into every living being created in the Waters of Nun. Uranus is clearly responsible for hundreds, if not thousands, of deaths. This is why his power has been stripped from him."

Gaia's arm crumbles off, but in her concern, she pushes him further. "Why were we not told?"

"I assumed you would complete the mission without deviation," Nun responds, a cold aura emanating from his eyes.

Though her anatomy is resistant to the sensation of pain, the eventual breakdown of her limbs is inevitable. Gaia presses forward. "I must continue—even now as my body erodes."

She again Inhales deeply, further depleting her energy reserves. "With his power stripped from him, he fell into madness," she says, her voice growing fainter. "He said he needed to consume the power of our children!"

Nun nods. "A catalyst...Even with no knowledge of our home planet's culture, your husband instinctively knew that."

Gaia doesn't care for the explanation. She continues, "Regardless of what a catalyst is, I couldn't let this go on anymore. I took my eldest son, Cronus, into my confidence. He saw the madness in his father's eyes and agreed to help bring him down. With the help of my kin, led by Cronus, we succeeded in slaughtering Uranus. Once complete, all that remained of him was his unbreakable core."

"The catalyst," Nun reiterates.

Gaia, severely weakened and fading, struggles to produce her final words. "Cronus took power and reigned over our homeland for many years. But as with his father, in time he grew tired of humans. He considered himself a liberator and used Uranus's core to create species unknown to Earth. After their proliferation, Greece was overrun, and soon Cronus suffered the same fate as his father. Unlike his father, however, he did consume his children's cores upon their birth. His wife, Rhea, pleaded with me to fix this..."

Gaia falls backward as her weight becomes unsteady. She falls with enough force to shatter her singed skin. The neon-green jade of her core glows through the countless cracks as what's left of her body slowly sinks into the ground.

Melting. Draining.

Nun kneels down to her withered form. He reaches out instinctively but stops himself before touching her, remembering the flames. "It is a sad fate, but why come to me?" He asks. "You know I cannot leave. Why not go to the others I sent forth?"

Gaia angrily replies, "Because they all have fallen! Every last one of them has become corrupted by their inherent power."

Nun's usual blue aura fades to a piercing white. He stares blankly at Gaia before turning away. She watches as his body glows a burning red aura, and he clenches his fists. He yells, "This is a disgrace! How could this happen?"

Gaia gives a soft smile. She explains her meaning. "Father...this is not your fault. There is something fundamentally wrong with immortality and power. There may be no hope for the ones before, but you can create a new being. One that rivals my own."

Nun shakes his head in disagreement. The revelation of the horror his kin has wrought upon the world in his absence weakens his resolve. In his mind, there is no way forward.

But Gaia pleads, and in reluctance, Nun lets her explain her vision. "I believe the next generation should be no different in mortality than the humans you wish for them...to r-r-r-rule ov-ov-over." Gaia stutters due to the erosion of her once-alluring face. She continues, "I have seen th-the humans. Their fear of death quells the e-ego. And when they do s-something heroic, they weigh their life against it and deem it a worthy cause."

Gaia's wise words rekindle the slight spark of hope that

remains within Nun. It is as if she has revealed the secret to the human psyche. This sense of renewal is plainly visible in his bright, glowing eyes.

Nun confirms, "Perhaps that is where I missed the mark—granting immortality. I must try again. But I shall not create as many this time around. I must control their numbers and train them slowly, cautiously, with great oversight so that they may remain grounded."

Gaia smiles as her smoldering body gives way. Her neck begins to crumble as her time nears its end.

"I believe you will succeed this time," Gaia says, leaving her last words of encouragement.

Nun grabs her crumbling hand from the ground before him, forsaking his caution of the flames. "Listen, child. I did not fail the first time," he explains. "I just made it too hard for your kind to succeed. Of all those who have failed, you seem to have done just fine. Are you not a success?"

It is a concept that Gaia had never considered until now. She responds with a choking whisper. "You speak the t-truth, father. Maybe there is hope for my family yet."

"Your time has passed, my child. Rest now," Nun says with cold blue eyes that betray his heartache.

Gaia's hand splinters into dust particles that cover Nun's hand. Her jade core melts and spills at Nun's feet, an ooze of neon green. All that remains of her crystalline form is a sliver of Jade—the sole portion of Gaia's body left untainted by the outside world.

Nun picks up the jade sliver and stands over the ashes of his most beloved daughter.

I wish I could have saved you, but this land was never meant for those who have been in the outside world. I shall pass your catalyst on to one deserving of it when the time is right.

Nun, angry over the latest revelations, summons the Eye of Oblivion to observe just what the sons of Nibiru have been up to these last one-thousand plus years.

In his resulting vision, he sees a grand complex built in the dry lands of the north, generating immense power. The Anunnaki have enslaved the locals and use them to mine the surrounding areas for resources to construct their massive energy facilities.

Nun cannot discern the actual reason for the construction, though he has seen things like this on his home world—structures that were created by fringe sects disloyal to the existential cause of the three races for a purpose that was never revealed in his time.

Could it be that the Anunnaki are direct descendants of these fringe groups from our home world? Could they somehow have corrupted my waters before I was awoken?

Unable to settle on an agreeable conclusion, he changes his focus to the Deva. To his surprise, the Deva are untraceable, though he does find the ruins of their original settlement.

He gasps at the sickeningly sobering sight. The land appears scorched, with structures toppled by generations of war. The sparse number of humans left behind appear malnourished and diseased.

Nun closes the Eye of Oblivion, unable to stomach more disappointment. His eyes return to the spot where Gaia's body disintegrated. He considers her words.

I am a fool. I should have used the Eye during the time of the Ancients, providing oversight. Then I might have seen their treachery before they ever departed. The Eye is but one of three great immortal souls of Nibiru. The other two are still missing, and if the Devas were to find them…

Nun quells his thoughts of a worst-case scenario. A moment of silence follows. Then he turns and heads back toward the massive lake in the middle of the Rift.

He reaches its shores, still mulling over Gaia's philosophy. He studies the churning liquid, dipping his hands into its dense flow. As Nun focuses his thoughts, he causes the water to flash in spurts of red. It crackles, electrified. Then, once imbued with specific instructions, the water returns to its translucent azure state.

Nun raises a hand skyward and calls forth the waters. "Waters of life, grant me a human child. Give it the powers of an Ancient, the mortal lifespan of a man. Bestow it with both weaknesses and strengths. May it need before it ever wants. It must be that of this world. I command you now. Bring it unto me!"

The water's many elements coalesce, forming a vortex around Nun's submerged hand. In the whirlpool beneath his fingers, a figure appears in the shape of an infant child. It takes the form of water, then metal, then—finally—flesh.

Nun curiously observes the child before him. He's never viewed one this close, having crafted his prior creations in their full form.

With tremendous care, he scoops the child from the waters—humanity in the palm of his hand. The child takes its first breath of life but remains asleep.

Nun uses the garbs from his cloak to keep the child warm and swaddles it, contemplating the future.

The Eye of Oblivion senses his wandering thoughts and opens on its own. Nun attempts to stop it, but to no avail. He is aware of its goal, one that could prove very dangerous. The Eye, given its own sentience, refuses to be stopped. It projects to Nun a vision of the future.

An Empire…Three Kings…Megalithic architecture…Massive armies of men…Major world-shaping disasters…Millions dead…

Nun responds in terror. "What is this?"

The Eye closes, leaving the vision to exist only within his mind. He looks down at the child.

Could it be he who will change the fate of the world? Surely he could not lead the world to such ruin.

Nun immediately forces himself to block all knowledge of this vision from his psyche.

Visions of the future are fraught with danger. They haunt the deeper recesses of the subconscious, shaping everyday decisions in failed attempts to avoid that which one only draws closer. No. This boy's destiny is his and his alone. So shall it be.

Nun speaks softly to the boy, "You shall be raised as a human." He pulls the child closer to his face. "You will not be the only child I raise, but you shall be the first. I shall call you Rah, son of Nun—the first of the God Killers."

3 DECISIONS

Twenty years pass since Gaia's sacrifice and Nun's creation of Rah.

The evening sun slowly sinks across the sky above the Rift. An alien pyramid structure stretches toward white clouds and blue skies above. At its peak, a metallic protrusion produces electric sparks that flicker in sporadic zaps as if from a Tesla Coil. The electric current casts all that surrounds it with a shimmering scarlet glow. Nun's laboratory. It's surrounded by a lush forest here in the eastern area of The Rift.

To the north lie the Flats. There, temperatures frequently peak upward of one hundred degrees. The arid terrain serves as a training ground for the mortals of Nun's creation. It is here that our story begins, as a long day's practice comes to an end.

Perched on a boulder, Rah watches intently as Apedemak spars with Bydos, who charges at him with a sharp spear.

Apedemak waits until Bydos is within leg's length then sidesteps and delivers a kick to Bydos's rib.

"You must focus on more than my shoulders," Apedemak says. "Legs are weapons that reach much farther than arms."

Bydos is stunned by the force. He stifles a whimper as he rolls into the sand, dropping his spear. Using the momentum to come up in one motion, he grabs his shield resting against the boulder where Rah sits.

He moves swiftly and crouches behind the boulder, listening for Apedemak's footsteps for what seems like an eternity.

They come from his left. Bydos feels his adrenaline kick in. Though he knows Apedemak will not inflict mortal harm, Bydos revels in this rush of hormones. His breathing quickens in response as Apedemak nears.

Just before Apedemak can catch a glimpse of him, Bydos rushes around to the right of the boulder. Apedemak doubles back and spots Bydos retreating to gain distance. He hurls a spear toward Bydos, who looks up just in time to hoist his shield in front of his face. The spear lodges deep within its wooden surface.

Bydos stands his ground, struggling to free the spear as Apedemak walks toward him, looking for the first opportunity to strike. He takes his time, slightly worn after hours practicing in the heat. Still, he will not relent, not even for his younger sibling.

Bydos knows this as he wrests the spear free from his shield and throws it toward Apedemak, who tucks and rolls out of the way.

"Enough! We're losing the light," Rah says as he stands. His metallic neckpiece bounces the last of the sun's rays into Bydos's eyes.

Apedemak stands, raises a hand, and looks at the sky swathed in shades of orange, violet, and magenta. He throws his javelin into the dirt, but his spear doesn't leave his hand.

Bydos lowers his shield and gives Apedemak a questioning look.

Apedemak ruffles Bydos's hair. "A good performance, boy," he says. "You continue to improve rapidly."

Yes, but when will the day come that I can defeat you, my brother? It is of no use to have boundless skill if it still does not result in victory.

Apedemak stops as if he hears Bydos's thoughts. He

places his hands on the boy's shoulders, a gleam of pride in his eye, "In time..."

"In time, in time, in time! Is no one else around here sick of hearing that?" a nettlesome voice says playfully.

Apedemak and Bydos look up to see Gilgamesh stalking across the training ground, his face replete with its usual cocky smirk. The tufted fabric of his royal blue Sumerian robe blows in the wind as he approaches Rah.

"In time perhaps you will learn the virtue of patience," Rah says coldly. His serious demeanor couldn't be more opposite that of the mischievously playful Gilgamesh. The two constantly grate each other's nerves, with only Gilgamesh seeming to enjoy the tension.

Rah reminds himself of this as Gilgamesh walks up and jabs him in the chest with an index finger, tauntingly. "Patience?" He scoffs. "That's what you call rolling around in the dirt day in and day out? I mean, what are any of us really learning anymore?"

Rah looks down at his outstretched arm. "Remove your hand, or I shall remove it *for* you."

Gilgamesh smiles. "I'm sure you will." He pushes his finger deeper into Rah's chest, pressing his face in close. "You're perfectly content as long as you can lord over this comfortable little prison cell we call—"

Rah moves, closing a hand around Gilgamesh's forearm. With a slight flick of his wrist, Gilgamesh is tossed violently into the dirt before him.

Rah surveys the damage and then crosses his arms, dismissive. "You were warned." He stares Gilgamesh deep in the eyes. Only once he feels his admonishment has been properly received does he continue, "And never presume to know my mind. Ever."

Gilgamesh looks up, brushing the sand from his face. He flexes his arm and winces. *The brute is getting stronger. Perhaps the finger poke was a bit much. Next time, I'll just stick to the verbal taunts.*

"Nonetheless, you raise a valid point," Rah says. "I had wondered if it was finally time to venture beyond the Rift."

Gilgamesh opens his mouth to speak, but Rah silences him with a slow raise of his hand. "We will discuss this later."

Gilgamesh can't resist a smirk. *On second thought, that admission was actually worth a bruise or two.*

"Hey!" a distant female voice cries.

They look up and spot Amesemi jogging across the training ground toward them. With the sun at her back, she's a goddess in red, her bosom full, bouncing with each stride.

As she nears, they notice that the scowl on Amesemi's face matches her tone. "You were supposed to be back at the facility a half hour ago. We've received a beacon crystal message from Nun, and…" She notices their concerned expressions. "Why the long faces? What's happened?"

"Gilgamesh suggests it may be time we leave the Rift," Rah says. Amesemi stares at him as he takes his time forming his words. "I suspect I agree," he says with a nod.

"Agree? With him? Wonders will never cease," Amesemi says with a laugh, her locks billowing in the breeze.

Bydos looks up at Rah, worried. "You were serious? But…I don't think I'm ready, brother. Are any of us ready?"

Amesemi looks at Rah in shock. "Wait, you really think it's time to leave? *Seriously?*"

"We shall discuss this later," Rah says. "I need to be alone."

Rah stands in the shallows of the Waters of Nun. Its turquoise, oil-thick waters swirl in a perpetual counterclockwise motion around the towering wreckage of Nun's ship that juts skyward, challenging the sheer cliffs surrounding the landscape. The sun has set behind the mountains in the distance, but a kaleidoscope of colors still paints the evening sky.

High above, even more mountains hover in the sky— monolithic columns of stone suspended by some unknown magic, or perhaps Nun's advanced technology. But Rah thinks nothing of them. To him, that is simply the way of things. Here, mountains can hover, and waters such as the lake before him possess sentience.

Rah reaches down, takes a handful of the thick water, and splashes it on his face. *Agreeing with Gilgamesh...*He shakes his head in disgust. *And yet he does have a point. How much longer can Nun possibly have us wait?* He looks around, flexing his hands in question. *What is there left to learn, old man?*

"Secrets."

Rah flinches. The word is faint, but distinct—almost like someone muttering at the back of his mind. He had hoped he was rid of the voices, but time and again they return to provide equal parts wisdom and torment. Rah's voice drops to a savage whisper. "Get out."

"Secrets..." the voice whispers again, the word dissolving into a hiss.

Rah clasps the sides of his head with his hands as he treads further out into the water. "Get out of my head! Leave!"

The voice comes through clearly now. "We can't leave. Nun harbors secrets. Secrets of which you know nothing!"

Fear and doubt creeping in. It's just an attempt to prevent my venturing into the unknown. Rah thrusts his fists into the water, sending water spraying high into the air. "Oh? Should I force them to stay, then?" he yells. "Prove Gilgamesh right?"

His face darkens. How he despises this—the sense that he's arguing with himself, and worse, that the voices might be worth listening to. "No. No," he says aloud. He shakes his head as if it will fling the voices free from his mind.

"Secrets. Secrets. Secrets…"

He's tormented now, unsure if this is reality or illusion. *Nun has never let any of us into his facility besides Amesemi. What is he hiding? What is she?*

Enough! Rah screams, this time to himself. He's sweating beads now. Delirious. He growls and ferociously drops into a perfect combat stance, the water now at his chin. In swift, powerful motions, he moves from one form to another, striking the thick water.

"No…" the voice moans.

It's as if Rah's attacks are really hurting it somehow. Emboldened, Rah doubles down on his efforts. With each mighty blow, he unleashes a violent yell, causing the winds to rise.

His dissipation of energy disrupts the counterclockwise flow of the tide, creating large waves leading away from him. He senses his inner frustration being carried away from him like mist in the breeze.

He stops.

All is silent, apart from his heavy breathing. The torrential waves in the lake quickly settle back into their counterclockwise ripples.

Rah surveys the surrounding landscape, satisfied. *Good.* He turns and wades back to the beach.

A figure stands in the distance, high atop the cliffs that overlook the lake, watching him. Amesemi.

What is she doing? Has she come here for an audience? Are they all here?

"Show yourselves!" he yells as he walks ashore, thick clumps of water slowly oozing off his skin. His voice echoes off the surrounding cliffs, announcing itself to each nook and crevice.

There's a rustling in the dense but shallow forest that lies between Rah and the cliffside. It catches his attention. He turns to see Apedemak and Bydos emerging from the foliage.

Rah approaches them with purpose, a scowl on his face. *Very well…This is as good a time and place as any.*

Amesemi steps out of the forest, joining the others.

Rah looks from one to the other. "With whom should I speak first?"

***

Insects chirp in the night. Rah and Amesemi sit on a large, moss-covered boulder that juts from the ground. High above them, stars peek through the forest canopy.

A sliver of moonlight illuminates a narrow patch of grass. Apedemak and Bydos use it to spar, the clacking of their weapons mixing with the sound of leaves in the breeze. High above them, Gilgamesh climbs a tree, eager to explore the canopy.

"I can see clear across The Rift from here!" he yells. His movement causes a coconut to drop at Rah's feet. Rah picks it up and thumps it with little effort. It cracks open with ease. He takes half for himself and hands half to Amesemi.

"Would you join us, Amesemi, if we leave?"

Though his face doesn't betray his thoughts, even Rah has come to notice how lovely Amesemi has grown into her form. He studies the rich brown cocoa of her skin, the shape of her breasts pressing against her red shroud. He studies so long that he misses the first part of her response.

"...and besides, you're assuming that Nun would actually grant your request," Amesemi says as she scoops out a thick chunk of coconut flesh.

Rah looks at her curiously. "And why would he not?" He can hardly mask the distrust growing in his mind.

"I live with him, remember? I study under him," Amesemi says. "You have no idea how much emphasis he places on being ready—on learning things properly. Everything 'in due time.' Ugh." She shakes her head.

She takes another chunk of coconut, eating it as she thinks aloud. "Trust me. If he judges you're not ready, he'll hardly grant you the authority to walk away with such ease."

Rah nods. "And yet you sound as if it frustrates you, too." He eats a chunk of coconut flesh, waiting for Amesemi to fall into the trap he just set.

"A little, perhaps." Amesemi shrugs. "But...he knows things. You have no idea of the wisdom in that old man's library. The secrets. I doubt there's anything outside the Rift that could even compare."

Secrets!

Rah remembers the voices by the lake, and the scowls.

Amesemi cocks her head to the side, curiously. "What is it?"

"Nothing," Rah says with a dismissive wave of his hand.

"And there's that. You're not the most diplomatic of men, are you?" Amesemi questions. "Not much for discussion." She pauses. "Do you actually think you could hold this little band of ours together the way you are, out there? Your temper, Gilgamesh's pride...we'd be scattered to the winds within days."

Off to the side, Apedemak cuts his eyes in their direction. Seeing them alone, Amesemi so comfortable in the brute's presence, eats at him. He lets his gaze linger a tad too long, allowing Bydos to score a swift chop to his obliques. Apedemak raises his hand, calling it quits to the night's impromptu sparring session.

Rah takes in Amesemi's words. "Hmmm." Eating gives him time enough to think. He's still unsure if she can be trusted, but he senses an opening. One more test. He looks Amesemi dead in her eye. "So your decision is no, then?"

"For the moment," Amesemi says, fully resolved.

For the moment. She didn't rule it out completely. Maybe she isn't totally sworn in allegiance to the old man.

Apedemak and Bydos stroll over, sweaty and heaving for breath.

Rah turns to Apedemak. "And you. Are you ready for the world outside the Rift?" he asks.

Apedemak hides his surprise at the question just hurled at him. *Outside the Rift? He and Gilgamesh are taking this more seriously than I imagined.* "Oh, I am. But are you?" Apedemak asks, confidently hiding his angst.

Rah raises an eyebrow. "Is that a joke? I am the strongest one here. You have firsthand experience of —"

"You think that's going to be enough?" Apedemak asks, his frustration building. "There are millions of people out there beyond the Rift, remember? Each of them living their own lives, nursing their own dreams, working toward their own goals." He steps closer to Rah. "You think you can bring them together with strength alone? Do you want to rule through fear?"

"It can be done." Rah shrugs.

Apedemak shakes his head in disapproval. "Perhaps it can. But should it be? What of honor, or compassion? You think you can be a leader without caring for those you lead?"

Rah shrugs, seeing absolutely nothing wrong with Apedemak's proposed totalitarianism.

Apedemak sighs. "Sometimes I wonder if you'll ever understand these things."

Rah looks at Apedemak, insulted. "I was looking for your opinion, but I can surely beat some respect into you if you'd prefer—"

"You keep saying that sort of thing, brother, and yet you never seem to ask yourself why you've had no success as of yet," Apedemak snaps at him.

He's got him, and he knows it. It's the one thing that eats away at Rah. He could beat Apedemak to a pulp, and he'd still never submit. Surely no human on the outside could withstand such a beating…but what if they could? Would they rise up against Rah? *Is it enough to rule through fear alone?*

The leaves above them begin to rustle, interrupting his thoughts. Rah stands suddenly. "Enough. We don't have time for this. Not here, not now."

He steps toward Apedemak. "But…if the opportunity presented itself, you would leave, then?"

Apedemak sighs, "For what it's worth, yes. I would leave."

Rah is surprised. He didn't expect Apedemak to side with him, especially after Amesemi's earlier protest. *Perhaps he could be used to sway her. Then, she could convince Nun. But then, what if she were to change Apedemak's mind and he no longer—*

Gilgamesh drops down from the tree above, diverting Rah's attention from the contemplation of infinite unknowns. He wipes off his arms and extends his hand toward Rah.

"Figured I'd drop down to accept your apology."

"*Apology*? I've offered you no such thing," Rah says with disdain. How dare Gilgamesh derail his train of thought.

Gilgamesh smiles broadly. "I understand. Truly, I do; it's hard to admit you were in the wrong. But cheer up! We're leaving!"

Rah stares at Gilgamesh's outstretched hand until he retracts it. His lighthearted demeanor and silly smile never fail to boil Rah's blood. "*You* seem excited," Rah says flatly.

"Why wouldn't I be?" Gilgamesh thrusts a celebratory fist into the air. "Freedom! Adventure! Limitless opportunities!" He leans in and places his hand on Rah's shoulder. "You know, you should pay more attention to Nun's archives, brother. Do you have any idea how they'd treat us out there? Such exemplary specimens of humanity?"

Rah ponders upon this. *Hmm…perhaps I should spend more time in Nun's library. The archives are the one place where I may be able to find more about these secrets of his.*

Gilgamesh flexes his muscles, smiling at himself as he continues, "We're stronger than them—smarter, more handsome…" He looks at Rah askance. "Well, some of us more so than others." He points toward Bydos sharpening his spear on the boulder Amesemi and Rah sit on. "Why, even the brat could surpass half the armies of the world single-handedly!"

Rah looks at him, unamused. "Your point?"

Gilgamesh laughs and places his arm around Rah's shoulders. The swift flicker of Rah's eyes warn Gilgamesh to tread lightly.

"Don't you see? We could live like kings out there. Riches! Wine! Women! They'd be falling all over you, I'm sure," Gilgamesh says as he gives Rah a forceful pat on the back. "With those strong, manly arms and that brooding aura of yours," Gilgamesh teases, squeezing Rah's arm. "Such things are quite popular, or so I hear. So many things to see, to do." He looks up, waving his hands in wonderment. "And to have done *to* me..." His voice trails off at the thought.

"Well then, your mind is made up, I suppose?" Rah asks.

Gilgamesh chuckles. "And yours isn't?"

"Hedonism for its own sake does not hold quite the same appeal for me," Rah says with a shrug.

"Oh. No, I suppose it wouldn't." Gilgamesh looks Rah up and down. "Not to worry. I'm sure you'll find plenty of things out there you can punch very hard," he says with a playful smile.

Unable to bare anymore, Bydos stabs his spear into the ground in frustration. "You guys are really planning on leaving?" To him, such talk smacks of betrayal. And then there's the fear. *What would happen if they left?*

Rah turns toward him. "Does the idea of leaving still concern you? What's there to worry about? We would protect you, boy."

Bydos thinks for a moment before he answers. They already think of him as weaker. He can't admit his apprehension, so he lies. "Not so much. It was nerves, I think. To hear you talking about it out of the blue. But I keep hearing that I'm improving."

Bydos nods toward Apedemak. "He makes it sound as if I could be stronger than all of you, someday."

Rah smiles at Bydos in amusement. "Does he now?"

The boy flushes. "I don't—I didn't mean it like that. Honestly. I'd never seek to cross you, brother." He looks around at the others. "*Any* of you. I...I like being a soldier. I find it easier to take orders than to give them. I don't think that has to be a bad thing, does it?"

Rah pats him on the back, "I suppose not. You're wise beyond your years sometimes, boy. I would be glad to take you with us, if that is what you want."

Bydos nods. "It is." He knows it's a lie, but perhaps in time, it will turn into a truth. He cuts his eye at Amesemi, who sits with her arms crossed, rolling her eyes at all of them, and he immediately wishes he'd said nothing.

***

The four of them arrive at the western side of the Rift, where a complex of stone buildings surrounds a courtyard. This is their living quarters.

There's an armory, a food repository, sleeping quarters, and the library, where Nun houses his archives and his lab.

They make their way through the courtyard toward the sleeping quarters, dodging a massive crater in the ground.

"So the die is cast. I would not force anyone to leave, but it seems most of us want to. As such, I shall leave at first light to go speak with the old man," Rah says before turning to Gilgamesh. "I must be expeditious. Lend me your horse."

Gilgamesh is taken aback by the request. His eyes bug, and he looks horrified at the mere suggestion. "Oh, no. Fadesh stays with me."

It's a damn horse. Why must he always be so petty? Rah clenches his fist and scowls at Gilgamesh. "Must you always be a petulant child?"

"You're actually prepared to fight me for him," Gilgamesh says to Rah in disbelief. "Horrible."

Rah frowns at Gilgamesh, imagining thirteen different

ways to smack that annoying smirk from his face.

Sensing the increasing tension, Amesemi gestures toward the crater caused days ago by another innocent comment turned all-out brawl. "Please," she says, "the more damage you create wrestling with your egos, the more time we must spend repairing the facility. We have much to do if we are to depart soon."

"Indeed, some of us can find much better use of our time," Apedemak says, smiling at Amesemi.

It's a smile Amesemi's come to appreciate more lately. While Rah is too aggressive and Gilgamesh too callow, Apedemak reminds her of the old man. Stoic and strong, but capable of exercising intellect.

She turns away without a response. *So many things could be a much better use of time.* She glances at **Apedemak's muscular physique.** *If only the others weren't here with us right now.* She turns her head, biting her lip at the thought.

Apedemak's smile fades as Amesemi turns away. *Why is it that I cannot connect with her? Each time I try, nothing. If only I didn't have to contend with these idiots. Just she and I alone could forge a much stronger connection.*

As they reach their sleeping quarters, Rah is still fixated on Gilgamesh. Now, annoyed by his cocky saunter through the courtyard, Rah studies him for physical weakness. *I could easily sweep his underdeveloped legs from under him and have him pleading in submission before his back got dirty...A fight. Hmmm...it is tempting. But to spoil such a momentous decision...*

He reconsiders his thought and shrugs. "Very well. Keep your beast. I can travel to Nun's laboratory and back on foot," Rah says as Gilgamesh spins around.

"Still on that, are we?" Gilgamesh says with his usual grin.

Rah continues, "We've waited long enough; another day is hardly that much more to bear. I shall leave tonight." They walk inside, each pondering the outcome of Rah's journey.

The Road Ahead—Rah's Personal Journal

The time has finally come. Tonight I set off for Nun's facility to request him to allow us to leave the Rift and grant the five of us our freedom. I doubt I shall actually arrive until midday, as Gilgamesh would not loan me his horse, and we have no other suitable mount. Still, hopefully the journey proves uneventful. I hope too that Nun sees the sense in our request. This place has nothing left to offer us. We should leave, and we should leave now!

4 FRUSTRATIONS

It's the early-morning twilight, the hour of the wolf.

Nun's massive pyramidal laboratory is noticeably quiet; its usual electric cackle is reduced to a soothing hum that permeates the forest that surrounds it.

The lake, too, lies eerily still. In its center, foliage grows from the three-pronged legs that surround a massive propulsion outlet on Nun's crashed ship in the middle of the lake. The birds that usually nest inside the propulsion outlet are noticeably absent this morning. Behind the ship, dawn is merely a strip of golden light on the horizon.

Gilgamesh leads his brown horse, Fadesh, carefully down the cliffside toward the shore. He rides quietly, a slight smile on his face as he hums to himself. This is the kind of morning he lives for. The tranquil dawn of a new day bringing with it infinite possibilities—infinite adventure.

Gilgamesh has never been much for sleeping, anyway, getting only a few hours a night, if any. Today he plans to head toward one of his favorite spots in the mountains of the northwest quadrant of the Rift. It's a place the others have yet to venture, and he prefers it that way.

Alone in mountainous solace, Gilgamesh can wipe away his ever-present smile and ponder the complexities of existence.

His existence. The others'. The Rift. The outside world.

Thoughts of life outside plague him more and more with each passing day. He finds the presence of the others to be increasingly claustrophobic. Their constant bickering—Rah with his anger, his sickness; Apedemak and his embarrassing, if silent, pining for Amesemi. Sure, Bydos is fine, but in time he may lose his acquiescing personality, becoming another thorn in Gilgamesh's side.

The outside world—it becomes more tempting with each and every thought.

Fadesh trots down an embankment and comes to a clearing. Gilgamesh stiffens suddenly, realizing he is not alone. He pulls tight on the reins, bringing his mare to a stop.

Apedemak crouches by the water's edge, gazing out into the morning. He comes here often to meditate. A good leader must have a clear focus, must learn to detach himself from emotions, from longings. Apedemak has long been aware of this; however, this morning he finds it impossible to still his mind.

Increasingly, his thoughts have come to center around Amesemi. He can't seem to get a read on her intimate thoughts the way he can with the others. Like Nun, she is impenetrable in that way. Still, she always seems to be preoccupied with Rah and Gilgamesh—mediating their conflicts, worrying for their well-being. Despite this, Apedemak senses a commonality between the two of them. They both are, after all, the more mature and logical of the group.

Apedemak chuckles at the thought of he and Amesemi being the parents to three unruly adults. His mind then imagines something deeper—he and Amesemi locked in embrace. His hand upon her growing stomach. Apedemak teaching a wiry little boy, theirs, how to fashion a spear.

Somehow these thoughts have come to take precedence over his previous aim of usurping Rah as the leader of their contingent. *Let him satisfy his ego. He shall either rise to the occasion or be torn asunder by his own rage. All I desire is Amesemi.*

He considers the journey ahead and decides that he will not depart the Rift until she does. And when that time comes, he will do all within his power to ensure that they venture into the outside world together.

Having taken in the moment, he stands and turns toward Gilgamesh.

What is he doing out this early?

"I was meditating," Apedemak says, reading Gilgamesh's thought that echoed his own.

Gilgamesh throws up his arms, incredulous. "Can't a man have anything to himself around here? Not even one's thoughts are sacred between you and Nun."

"You said nothing of going anywhere today," Apedemak says, regarding Gilgamesh with a weary expression.

"Because," Gilgamesh says with a slight frown, "you would have tried to stop me."

A warm voice calls out behind them, "I wonder why."

Gilgamesh turns to see Amesemi walking through the trees with Bydos close behind.

Of course! Neither Bydos or Apedemak are ever far from Amesemi. And who does she think she is anyway? Her time with Nun has given her an air of influence lately...and I don't like it.

Gilgamesh rubs the bulge between Fadesh's eyes, and the horse bends its front legs. Gilgamesh bows to Amesemi mockingly, his playful smile hiding his frustration at the interruption to his plans.

"Well, well, well. If it isn't little sister coming to be Nun's mouthpiece," Gilgamesh says as he taps the horse so it stands once more.

Amesemi is unamused. Her face is cold, scrutinizing. "Rah has yet to return, and you're choosing now, of all times, to run off and play?" She questions. "You do remember that he has ventured to Nun's per our request?"

He shrugs his shoulders, indifferent. "However I choose to spend my free time is of my concern, and—"

"Give him time to return with an answer," she says, her eyes squinting in growing fury.

Gilgamesh's impatience grows. "Yes, but how many more days must I wait?"

"You have all the patience of a fly. It has not even been one full day yet," Amesemi says, shaking her head.

Gilgamesh forces a yawn. "And yet…I'm bored," he says as he places his hands on the saddle of his horse. "Just think! Out there, in the world beyond the Rift, there's a new land to be discovered. New experiences to chase, adventures upon which I can feast," he says with fire in his eyes.

The others stare at him as a parent does a whimsical child. They move in front of his horse.

Bydos makes the first attempt at reason. "We'd be better served venturing out together, not one by one. With Rah gone, if you leave…" his voice trails off.

"Is it that serious? I'm merely going off on an adventure here in the Rift. You all make it seem as if I'm leaving for good."

"Yes, but Rah could be back any moment with confirmation," Apedemak remarks.

Gilgamesh is undeterred. "Confirmation, or strong rebuke. Who knows which way Nun's inner tide will swing at such a request. All I know is that I've tired of hanging on to the old man's every word. 'In due *time*.' I say the time is now *due*." He flexes his muscles, full of vanity. "Why, imagine—a man as strapping as I, forced to ask permission for the slightest request as if I were still a weeping little child." He cuts his eyes at Bydos, who doesn't notice.

Gilgamesh backs Fadesh up and makes him trot around the three others. "I'll leave it to you three to waste youth and vitality waiting for orders while Nun sits in his laboratory for eons, toiling away with who knows what." He stops beside Apedemak and bends down to his ear. "A real man finds it impossible to stifle the call of adventure."

Apedemak brushes off Gilgamesh's comment and shrugs in resignation. "And if you're still gone upon Rah's return?"

Gilgamesh shrugs his shoulders, "Umm...then you wait until I return, obviously. Is that so hard?"

Apedemak locks eyes with Gilgamesh. "I must warn you, little brother, should I have to waste time tracking you down, I guarantee to make your return rather unenjoyable."

Gilgamesh steps down from his horse, faces Apedemak, and smirks. "Beware the threats of a mighty warrior." He rolls his eyes. "Though I find it interesting, your posturing. Is this not the sort of behavior you condemn in Rah?" He shakes his head for effect. "Oh, the hypocrisy."

Amesemi's heard enough. "Grow up, and think of someone other than yourself for once, Gilgamesh. If we can't operate as a group now, how will we ever in the outside world? Your level of immaturity and lack of reasoning never cease to amaze me. At times it's as if Apedemak and I are the only sensible adults here."

Apedemak smiles at her admission and cocks his head toward Gilgamesh with a scornful eye.

Gilgamesh rolls his eyes. "You know, your posturing might be more effective if your source weren't a child."

Bydos scowls and casts his eyes downward as he shuffles.

Gilgamesh cuts his eyes toward Bydos and scoffs. "So it was you who betrayed my whereabouts." Without warning,

Gilgamesh cracks his whip at Bydos's feet. Bydos jumps back, instinctively grabbing his spear.

"Surely you're not as foolish as you are young. A *spear?*" Gilgamesh scoffs. "Amesemi was raised to be Nun's spy, and now she's enlisted you to join the coalition, I see."

He looks at Amesemi with a spiteful scowl. "And *this* is what you call operating as a group? Spying on me doing nothing more than enjoying my usual morning routine. Sometimes I'm not sure that you ever have a thought for yourself that wasn't given birth to by Nun. Perhaps you're more than just his little—"

"Enough," Apedemak roars in Amesemi's defense.

"And you," Gilgamesh says to Apedemak, "if you're going to be a man, learn to do so at all times, not just when *she* is threatened."

"Hey!" Bydos snaps. "I think you're being a bit unfair. All we've asked is that everyone remain close until Rah returns. Why the anger?"

Gilgamesh looks at Bydos with a mixture of surprise and outrage. "Growing a pair now, are we, boy?"

"I am no longer a child. I am becoming a man," Bydos asserts, standing his ground.

Gilgamesh snarls. "Then perhaps we'd learn to treat you as more than a mere child if you didn't go whining to your elders at a moment's notice." He turns back to his horse and hoists himself onto the saddle. "The next time you have concerns about my adventures, I suggest that you approach me one-on-one like a man, *boy.*"

"Okay, fine. Rushing beyond our normal boundaries within the Rift carelessly will only spell disaster," Bydos says.

Amesemi nods in agreement. "Exactly!"

Apedemak chuckles. "It's apparent that even a *child*

possesses more wisdom than you."

"And I possess more courage than the lot of you combined," Gilgamesh retorts. "As such, I assure you, there's no cause for worry." He nods at Amesemi. "While you find solace in Nun's sanctuary..." He waves his hand toward Apedemak and Bydos, "and you two in endless sparring on the Flats, it's within these uncharted crevices of the Rift that I find my nirvana."

Apedemak's hair coils. He takes a moment, absorbing the information it provides before he speaks. "There is a great tide of change on the horizon. Today would not be the best day to venture far. This I know."

Gilgamesh scoffs. "This you *know?* Oh, let me guess, your magic hair? You guys are overreacting. I'd be halfway there already, had you not interrupted my morning saunter. Thanks a lot, *boy*," he says to Bydos.

"Bydos just may have saved your skin by informing us," Amesemi says as she places her arm around Bydos's shoulder.

Gilgamesh snarls and digs his heels into the Fadesh's side, causing him to raise up on its hind legs and spin around until they face east. He stops and looks at the three of them, "You all reek of fear. Sit around waiting all day if you like. I'm off. Nun's decision will remain the same until I return. Perhaps by then you all will have mustered up a sense of courage that allows you to stand independent of the will of Nun."

Gilgamesh pulls tight on the reins. "Yah!" he yells, and Fadesh canters off down the shoreline.

Bydos stares at the dust left in his wake, his mouth open as he searches for words that seem to come to Amesemi with ease.

"Self-centered, thoughtless fool," Amesemi hisses

through her teeth as she turns and storms back toward Nun's towering pyramid facility. "May today be the day that he discovers humility," she says to herself.

Apedemak follows behind her. "Amesemi!" He quickly catches up to her and matches her pace. "Where are you going?"

"From the cliffs I can see which direction he goes in, just in case," Amesemi says without looking at Apedemak.

Back on the shore, Bydos shakes his head. "They're all prisoner to their emotions, yet *I'm* the one viewed as a child." Bydos chuckles to himself. He bends down, grabs his shield, hoists his spear from the sand, and reluctantly follows them into the woods.

***

They climb a sheer cliff overlooking the waters below. Apedemak attempts to calm Amesemi, who is a few feet ahead of him. "You mustn't let Gilgamesh's thrill for adventure upset you, nor fears of us all venturing beyond. Nun must have known this day would come. Surely, it's all a part of some larger plan of his," he says.

Amesemi turns toward Apedemak, her eyes ablaze as she reaches for a new foothold. "Well then, you be the one to tell him that both Gilgamesh and Rah plan a mutiny if he disagrees to let us leave."

The words send shockwaves through Apedemak's being. *Surely they wouldn't go without the old man's approval. And what of Amesemi and me? Will Nun take it as betrayal that I too feel ready to venture beyond?*

Amesemi continues to vent as she reaches out her hand, grabbing a small handhold. "I will not be held account—"

The piece of rock breaks off in her hand. She lets out a scream as she tumbles down toward Apedemak. He reaches out to catch her, but her momentum causes his other hand to lose its grip.

Together, they tumble down the face of the cliff, past Bydos, who quickly scales sideways to avoid their trajectory.

Midair, Apedemak wills himself to pick up speed. He reaches Amesemi, wrapping himself around her as his body tears through tree limbs. The two land in a heap on the ground, the force of their bodies leaving a small crater in the morning-dew-covered grass.

Amesemi stirs and rolls off of Apedemak. A decent climber, her first fall has shaken her.

Anger. It can cause one to fall. Literally, figuratively...

After a moment, Apedemak moves. "Are you okay?" Apedemak asks as he picks leaves from Amesemi's locks. She dusts herself off. Apedemak stands and extends his hand to help her up.

"I'm fine," Amesemi says, her eyes narrowed in feigned contempt.

"That was amazing," Bydos remarks as he climbs down from the cliffside, interrupting the awkward tension brewing between Apedemak and Amesemi.

Apedemak pays Bydos no attention as he dusts himself off and stares at Amesemi. "I thought I'd hurt you, and—" He extends his hand and helps her up.

"Hurt me?" she asks.

Apedemak realizes he's still holding her hand. *Wow. They're so soft—small.*

He meets her eyes and instantly becomes nervous, stammering. "Yes, well—you were, I just thought..." His voice trails off along with his thoughts.

"You shouldn't think so highly of yourself," Amesemi says as she takes her hand back and turns to walk toward the facility.

Bydos follows, leaving Apedemak alone with his thoughts.

As Amesemi begins to scale the wall again, she questions the surge of emotions and energy that coursed through her while in Apedemak's grasp. She's not been around the others for long, and this level of engagement is still new to her. Did she let on to just how much she enjoyed his touch? Surely not. *I can't; I mustn't. He cannot know when I'm vulnerable.*

"I'll keep watch out here," Apedemak booms from behind, derailing her train of thought.

Amesemi keeps climbing, her eyes studying the wall before her. "As you wish," she says nonchalantly. *Does he know my thoughts? How could he possibly?*

"I'll race you to the top," Bydos teases, as he looks over at a distracted Amesemi, his shield thrown over his back.

From the ground below, Apedemak watches them climb with enough competitive force to make the wall tremble. He clutches his fists in frustration at his sides. *All the strength of a lion reduced to nothing when I'm in her presence.*

He steps through the trees onto the shore and lets out the roar of a lion—a roar that wakes the entire canyon.

5 AN ANCIENT TEMPLE

An Ancient Temple—Rah's Personal Journal

I take note outside our father's home. This place…the ancient facility where Nun resides, is dark and silent. The wilderness grows high over its walls, yet, I sense life deep inside it—an ominous presence of considerable power. Never in all my days have I taken a single step over the threshold. Always, I stopped just before this still and lightless corridor. But there is a first time for everything.

***

The still of night. Nun's pyramid facility looms high above the towering canopy of trees. The electricity sparking from its peak glows against the dark night sky.

Deep inside, Rah walks through a dark corridor toward Nun's chambers. He knows Nun received his request for a meeting but Rah is also well aware that the old man has no need to honor said request. He hopes his lengthy travel is not in vain.

He enters a dark chamber. It's the deepest he's ever been allowed to go into Nun's facility. Around him, celeste-toned alien crystals the size of large boulders pulsate. They emit a strange energy as if they are breathing, further heightening Rah's anxiety.

What are these things? They're similar to the beacon crystals, but much larger.

Rah turns toward the eerie slicing sound of a large door opening. *What the—*

A slab of the onyx wall behind him descends into the

floor. Rah stands transfixed—these walls are massive; they are a couple of feet thick. He wonders what other hidden chambers lie within this sanctuary.

Suddenly, the sound of heavy footsteps announces Nun's arrival well before he enters the room. The structure trembles under his weight. It's enough to make even his boldest progeny tremble.

Rah instinctually backs a few steps away from the door, his reverence for the old man now obvious.

Nun enters the room. At almost ten feet tall, he's clad in a metallic suit of iridium and osmium. His eyes emit a piercing glow in the same celeste blue as the crystals surrounding the room.

"Father," Rah mumbles, more out of astonishment than greeting.

Nun's voice resonates through Rah's bones, causing them to vibrate as he speaks. "You seek an audience, boy? Unusual."

Rah's voice betrays his nervousness. He stammers, "M-my kin decided I would be the most fitting messenger to voice their concerns, father."

Nun's suit begins to glow, matching the chalky color of his eyes. In response, the crystals in the room begin to pulsate in a quickening rhythm, and the room lights up slowly, as if awakening from a slumber.

"Indeed. Come, then. Such a discussion should be held in private," he says before he turns and walks toward the door.

Rah studies the room in confusion. *In private? Who else could be here?* He notices the crystals in the room losing their light, returning to their slumber, as he follows Nun toward the corridor.

***

In the deeper recesses of the facility, Rah follows Nun at a respectful distance. For years he's wondered what lies within this structure, and now his eyes light up at the mysteries contained within.

Glowing electric discharge arcs across onyx walls. Lightning racing against the onyx emits crackles and pops with electric current. One arc of electricity catches Rah's eye. It lights up engraved inscriptions all along the wall. He dares to run his hand along a carving, unable to make it out. *Some alien language that only the old man knows.*

CRACK!

Another large spark of current nearby makes him jerk his hand back in reflex.

Suddenly all goes dark. Rah panics as his eyes adjust to the darkness. He searches for the dim light of Nun's suit. He staggers forward, toward the sound of massive footsteps, unable to see.

He walks into a wall. Curses! cautious arms feel for an opening. *He has to be around here somewhere. I would have heard a door.*

He feels an opening to his right. *The hallway.*

He turns to his left and focuses his eyes. Up ahead, he spots the faint glow of Nun's suit and hurries toward him.

Nun stops, and Rah stops at a safe distance behind him. *What's he doing now?*

"Step forward," Nun booms without looking back toward Rah.

Rah complies, and behind him, a thick slab of onyx rises from the floor, sealing off the corridor.

This place is a maze.

Rah senses a sudden vastness of space. Before him, Nun's suit begins to glow in increasing intensity as he gathers energy into himself. A hum rumbles from his suit. The glow from his hand awakens even larger crystals that buzz at the same frequency as his suit until the entire room hums with a palpable, living energy.

A crystal suddenly awakens behind Rah, causing him to jump forward in surprise. It floats, encased in a glass tube-like structure. Rah studies it with an innate sense that the crystal is sentient. More buzzing and humming sound elsewhere. The entire room is now illuminated with faint glows of white and azure blue bouncing off black walls.

He looks around, awed at the iridium and osmium-coated walls that rise seemingly into the dark night sky above with no end. Huge metallic columns rise throughout the room, electricity coursing through them visibly.

Dotting the room are even more massive alien crystals. A handful or so pulsate in a unique rhythm.

That sounds like…. a heartbeat?

Inside the crystals, large alien embryos of some sort lie frozen as the crystals pulsate in unison with Nun's breath as he watches Rah, expressionless.

"This place is quite the wonder!" Rah exclaims as his eyes continue studying the room.

"Indeed," Nun replies, quickly getting down to business. "So. You believe that the time has come, then?"

Rah flinches to hear his request stated so plainly. It's disconcerting to have his thoughts plucked from his brain in such a fashion. It's infuriating when Apedemak does it, but coming from Nun, it sounds like the pandering repetition of a naïve child's request.

In any other instance, Rah would meet the challenge of the question head-on. But with Nun, he would rather approach the subject in a more oblique manner.

"Are we not ready, father?" he asks.

Nun chuckles, his suit shimmering with ripples of yellow and orange light. "My dear son, you have no idea," he says with increasing laughter as he turns away from Rah, pacing unhurriedly across the floor. His laughter seems to ring unceasingly from wall to wall.

Rah bristles. "You find this amusing, old man? At first I thought to refuse their request. But now…I feel your arrogance has changed my mind."

"Really," Nun taunts. The light that spills from him turns a cool, distant blue.

He turns toward Rah and approaches with a crystal floating in his hand. Wrapped in a strip of iridium, the crystal pulses at the same rate as the room, like an organ torn from the corpse of some exotic creature. Amazed, Rah eyes it curiously.

Nun comes closer. "I understand why you and your kin wish to leave the Rift," he says. "Mortal as you are, such forced confinement must weigh heavy on your minds. But I cannot allow it." He pauses, letting his words sink in. Then he continues, "Not until you prove that you are ready."

Rah's anger erupts. "*Ready*? Our strength and ability are unmatched by any who would oppose us! Is that not proof?"

Nun takes his time before he answers. "If you truly believe that, you are not ready. Not in the slightest."

An awkward silence lingers in the air around him. Rah swears that the hum of the crystals has ceased. He begins to wonder if maybe he's said too much. Then, realizing that the old man can read his thoughts regardless, he proceeds. *Better to know exactly what you've communicated to the old man than to be left wondering what exactly he picked up on telepathically.*

"At times, I think you keep us imprisoned here for your own amusement. Or...maybe it's to assuage your sense of loneliness living in this dark, experimental tomb," Rah says.

He's never challenged the old man in this way before. In truth, he's never challenged the old man at all. Maybe it's the peeling away of mystery by stepping inside Nun's laboratory, or perhaps it's simply hubris. Whatever the reason, Rah feels more confident suddenly. Perhaps the old man will respect him more for speaking up.

Nun turns and walks away from Rah. He releases the crystal in his hand. It floats up toward the sky above, joining others scattered at various heights ahead and obscuring the ceiling.

Nun's inner radiance flares a dark and foreboding crimson that steals Rah's attention. "There are countless secrets in the Rift of which you know nothing about," he says with a tone of caution. "Some I kept hidden for your safety." He pauses. Then, "Some for my own."

He turns back toward Rah, this time with another crystal in his hand, amber colored. The crystal quakes violently. Rah studies the crystal curiously. "Wh-what is that?" he asks as the gem erratically bobs up and down above Nun's hand as if suspended in torrential waters.

"This is a Stability Gem," Nun explains. "Its sole purpose is to act as an anchor—to seal the faults created in the time of the Ancients and to keep the Rift from collapse— a task of paramount importance. *This* gem is the only reason why you yet live."

Rah stares at the throbbing crystal. In the back of his mind, he considers this story of Nun's.

Could it be true? The old man could tell me anything, and I wouldn't be the wiser. If only there were some way to know for sure.

Nun continues, "You ask what proof I could require?"

Rah bites his tongue in frustration as he reminds himself that thoughts are just as audible as spoken words in Nun's presence.

"Very well," Nun concedes as he brings his fingers together. Instantly, the crystal hovering above his hand disintegrates into countless tiny fragments that seem to dissolve into thin air.

What the—

The ground beneath them quakes vigorously, rocking the facility once more. This is much stronger than the smaller tremors before. It's enough to make an unsuspecting Rah lose his balance. He falls to his hands and knees, unable to rise.

Nun towers over him, serene, as though nothing has happened. Rah looks up at Nun, perplexed.

"Survive, then," Nun says. "for the next six months. All of you. Improve yourselves. Discover your hidden talents. Explore this place, the Rift. Learn the virtues of cooperation. After that time, I myself shall be your final test. This will be your proof...if you survive."

Nun's glow returns to its original cool celeste blue as the energy that poured from him fades.

A discombobulated Rah struggles to his feet in his greatest attempt to not show fear. *The old man acts as if the quake were nothing, but he sounded so sincere...*

He looks up to find Nun already disappearing through an exit that has just appeared within another section of the wall.

"Six more months," Rah mutters to himself. *In this prison? I shall go mad first. Surely I can surpass him, here and now.*

"Come," Nun beckons with a thundering voice.

Rah rises. Fear spikes in him momentarily as he questions if Nun was listening in on that particular thought. He exits the chamber just before the slab of rock seals the chamber and follows Nun through another corridor that looks similar to the first.

Nun continues his admonishment. "As to those who would oppose you, there are threats out there none of you could possibly imagine."

Behind him, Rah smirks at the thought of any man or creature besting him. *Surely the old man is delusional. Perhaps he is unaware of my true strength.*

Only after Rah's thoughts fade does Nun continue, "Creatures lurking in ruins from eons past that hunger to devour the fabric of your very being."

This must be hyperbole, why even if—

Nun stops and turns toward Rah with a piercing gaze. "Understand me. I shall rely on *you* to guide the others through these hazards. It is paramount that you are indeed ready to lead them, for you will need them in time. All of them," he says.

The frown on Rah's face delivers his response.

"You disagree?" Nun questions as the wall before them descends into the floor, revealing the quiet night outside the facility. He steps outside with Rah on his heels.

"I think you greatly underestimate me, old man," Rah says, his brewing impatience morphing to insolent anger. "Turn, face me!"

Nun spins around and finds Rah in a combat stance. "A challenge?" Nun lets out a hearty laugh that rustles the trees surrounding the facility.

Rah focuses, trying to silence his inner nervousness.

Nun strikes a combat stance of his own. "This was…unexpected." He nods toward Rah, beckoning him to attack. "Very well."

Rah centers every last bit of energy he possesses. He concentrates his power with enough force that the ground cracks beneath him as he changes his footing. He knows it will take everything he has to breach the old man's defenses. But he can do it. He can.

CRACK!

There's a large flash, the sound of lightning cracking.

He's struck Nun! Rah is amazed, but he knows he struck him.

But when he looks up, he sees his fist caught in the old man's hand. Rah's eyes go wide in shock.

Impossible!

The impact from that single blow sends a shockwave out for fifteen meters behind Nun, shattering the ground beneath him. A few trees in the forest just beyond lay slanted, their limbs splayed from the force.

And yet, the old man has caught it in his hand!

Rah looks up at Nun's face. His eyes glow a deep crimson as he begins to tighten his grip on Rah's fist. As the surge of pain begins to creep toward his chest, Rah feels a terror like none he has ever known.

"Well struck," Nun says as he tightens his grip still further. "Pointless. *Foolish,* mind you. But well struck."

Rah attempts to free his hand, but Nun's grip is unbreakable. He can hear the old man still talking, but the pain makes it hard for him to discern the words and their meaning.

"I applaud your sense of nobility, boy, but take care not to let it end up a millstone around your neck. At this point, the other purebloods would take your fledgling honor and break you with it."

Rah clenches his teeth from the pain. The pressure is starting to break his composure.

Must. Not. Show. Defeat.

Nun squeezes tighter still as he chastises, "But you can learn *if* you heed my teachings. Only then you might hope to stand against them, and maybe one day even defeat me in a fair fight."

Nun opens his hand. The dreadful, crushing pressure begins to abate, but Rah's hand and arm still throb in relentless pain. He staggers backward, clutching his wrist.

Worse than the physical pain is the burn of defeat. It's an entirely new feeling for Rah—one he'd rather not experience again.

Before him, Nun summons the Eye of Oblivion. It appears, hovering before them, and projects a hologram into the night air.

There's a shadow of Amesemi. "Amesmi's mastery of magic," Nun says.

The Eye conjures an image of Apedemak. "Apedemak's speed and resourcefulness."

Next is another hologram of Gilgamesh. "Gilgamesh's knowledge," Nun continues. "You will need them. You will need them all."

"I—I," Rah is too weak, too overwhelmed to form words.

"Even Bydos can be relied on," Nun continues. "The boy has incredible skills and an ability to learn any technique, shadowing you all."

With a flick of Nun's hand, the Eye of Oblivion disappears. Nun finalizes his thoughts. "Understand your people. A leader must do nothing less. Challenge them, lest they grow too comfortable." He steps in closer to Rah, who looks up at him in humble amazement.

"One day you stand to forge an empire, boy," Nun says. "Do not forsake your destiny."

And with that, Rah is calm. He sees it now. The training was merely the first step, with the real battle yet to come. His kin view him as a leader, and a true leader must lead by more than might alone. To claim their freedom will take a monumental effort, but what true prize is ever easily won?

Again, sensing his innermost thoughts, Nun steps close, placing his hand on Rah's shoulder.

"Forget your ego. Forget your wounded pride," he says as Rah looks into his glowing blue eyes. "For now, I am still your teacher—but in time, you will be a king."

Nun's Might—Rah's Personal Journal

He stopped my strike! I have no idea how, but he stopped my strike. I drew upon every last bit of power I possessed, and I couldn't even break his stance! We knew Nun was strong, but this? He told us the ancient bloodlines were his equals, give or take, and to hear the old man tell it, they numbered in the dozens at least! I assume he spoke the truth…What reason would he have to lie? But if that be the case, we have a serious problem.

6 FALSE UNITY

Nun and Rah sail across the thick waters of the lake on a large plate of solid onyx. This curious vessel has neither sail nor rudder, nor a motor of any kind. It responds only to Nun's telepathic commands. These commands, in tandem with the living waters of the lake, guide the vessel effortlessly.

Rah surveys the land around them as they travel. To the southwest, the wilds are engulfed in flames. He can hear the noise of great beasts fighting far in the distance, their roars and shrills unlike anything he's heard before.

"I thought I knew this place," Rah says, surveying the immense trees that lie broken and scattered around them. He wonders if they are returning in the same direction that he came. *Impossible. I would have noticed such destruction.*

"The Rift has changed considerably since the Ancient bloodlines walked here," Nun says, his tone reflective. "It cost me a great deal of effort to repair the damage they inflicted on it."

"Why is it you choose to bring me back to my quarters?" Rah asks, not understanding the connection between Nun's actions and his statement. "You said the only way we would survive your test was to learn self-reliance."

The charred remnants of foliage singe the hairs of Rah's nostrils. He tries unsuccessfully to stifle a cough.

Nun turns to Rah as the great disc glides across the lake. "It would have taken you days to return by yourself if you were travelling with all necessary caution," he says. His massive hand gestures a brush across the flame-engulfed environment as he continues. "Allowing you to travel alone would have most assuredly seen you dead before sundown. Now, there are far greater dangers than beasts and ancient ruins lurking here."

The great onyx slab twists around the bend in the lake. Nun continues, "Anomalies continue to warp the fabric of the Rift. And there are others out here lurking insidiously, powerful Ancients imprisoned centuries ago."

Rah studies his reflection in the dense waters below, trying to imagine these powerful Ancients.

Nun continues as if answering Rah's thought. "They have long since been forgotten, the passage of eons rendering them insane. Yet, with their powers, I doubt the lot of you could stand against even one of them. This is the reason I choose to escort you back—to keep you safe." Nun turns, facing forward to allow his words sink into Rah's psyche.

"That is one reason, but not the only reason, I take it," Rah says as he stares at Nun, who refuses to return his eye contact.

"Your safety is not my only concern. The others still know nothing of what transpired, or the changes yet to come. Likewise, I too am endangered. There were..." Nun's voice trails off as he stares ahead. Rah has never seen him like this—unsure, almost worried.

After a few moments lost to the sound of the waters beneath them, Nun continues, "There are things trapped beneath this realm. Beings of fearsome power that could overpower even me, if given the chance. I must see you home swiftly, then make a hasty return to my facility to reinforce it. I advise you to do the same with your own."

Rah struggles to process this unexpected confession. *The old man stopped my most powerful attack with ease, yet he fears these nameless creatures? This makes no sense.*

Then another thought occurs to him, and he looks up at Nun, furious.

"You knew if you broke that gem, these abominations might get loose, and that they could kill us—maybe even you?" he asks. "And yet you did it all the same?"

Finally, Nun returns his gaze toward Rah. "I had to see if my time with you and the others was worth it, whether I had truly prepared you for the chaos of the outside world. If you fail…" His voice trails off momentarily before resuming, "then I shall follow you to the grave. Not out of any special fondness for humanity—merely for the loyalty I have to my objective. Still…after all this time."

Rah stares at him, speechless.

"You are as strong as I could make a mere human, my boy, but that strength has taken its toll," Nun continues. "I'm aware of your struggle to contain your fractured psyche. It grieves me, even more so than you. I never imagined my gifts would have you pay such a terrible price. And yet you, Rah, are the only hope for your people."

Overwhelmed with cognitive dissonance, Rah attempts to push the old man's words to the back of his mind. He can see the shoreline fast approaching, and he has already begun to formulate a plan of action.

***

Stranger in My Own Land—Rah's Personal Journal

Everything I thought I knew has been cast asunder. The old man shattered one seemingly insignificant gem, and half the Rift is fell to pieces—the mountains struck down, the plains shaken apart, the forests in flames.

We were naive to assume that we could deal with whatever hazards lie outside the Rift. None of us is even prepared for what lies within.

From now on, we must measure each move we make. Caution must be our watchword—all of which is to say nothing of the ancient beings Nun claims the cataclysm set loose…The days to come will test us to our very limits and beyond.

It is Apedemak who spots Nun's onyx disc and its two passengers as he watches the lake by moonlight.

As if the surrounding cataclysm isn't enough to send shockwaves of anxiety coursing through him, Nun's presence compounds his worries further. Nun rarely ventures to this side of the Rift. For him to take time for a personal visit, the situation must be direr than even Apedemak imagines.

He tears off through the forest toward the sleeping quarters. There are still tremors rocking the landscape, aftershocks echoing the major earthquake that occurred just hours before. In the air, dark flurries of soot glide gently toward terra firma, covering the countryside in a thick, black suede.

In the distance, the night sky glows in warm colors, shades of ginger and garnet that pulsate intensely as lava explodes from a once-dormant volcano on the other side of the rift.

Apedemak carefully studies the ground, mindful of lava suppurating from newly opened fissures. A hodgepodge of incoherent thoughts bangs against the worry in his mind. He struggles to quell his fear.

***

It is predawn, just inside the barracks-like sleeping quarters. Each corner has been converted into its own sleeping area. Amesemi and Bydos are waiting in their respective areas.

Suddenly, Apedemak bursts through the door. "Rah has returned," he says, heaving to catch his breath.

Amesemi slowly rises, wipes her eyes, and stretches. "That was fast," she says with a yawn. Bydos rolls over and faces the door. His eyes swing toward Apedemak, full of apprehension.

"I see Nun with him too," Apedemak says.

Amesemi sits up straight in shock. "Nun?"

"Yes," Apedemak says with a nod. "The earthquakes have ravaged the landscape. I hope that Nun will be able to provide answers."

Amesemi stands and walks behind a shoulder-level wall where she changes into her usual attire. Apedemak turns his head away.

Bydos stands slowly. "What about Gilgamesh?"

Amesemi takes a few hurried steps toward the door and says, "We have to tell him Gilgamesh is gone."

This time she makes no attempt to conceal the worry in her voice, though she's not sure just what worries her so much. In truth, Gilgamesh has gone off daily. He was a rambunctious child, often disappearing for days in unexplored parts of the Rift before the age of ten.

He once climbed to the top of Nun's pyramid laboratory in an effort to touch the massive streaks of electric fire that sparked from its peak and flashed around the building like lightning. One touch and Gilgamesh was thrown a half a mile by the violent force of thousands of volts of negative energy.

No, it wasn't the fact that Gilgamesh had gone off that had her concerned. It was the nagging feeling that their entire lives up until now were on the brink of immense change.

So much had transpired within the last day—the realization that they are ready to leave the Rift. Amesemi had lied to the others. While she wasn't quite eager to leave, she had wondered recently what life on the outside could be like.

Then there was Rah's journey to see Nun. Was the old man returning to issue a stern rebuke? To keep them from leaving?

Not to mention the unprecedented seismic activity that shook the Rift to its very core in a literal sense. These were the thoughts that left little time for sleep the previous night, and now, the moment of truth has come.

Bydos is ready now. He stands, grabbing his shield and weapons. "Let's go," he says in an unusual display of leadership. He's the first to bolt through the door, leaving Apedemak and Amesemi staring at each other in surprise at his initiative.

"After you," Apedemak says as Amesemi walks past him with an extra sway in her step.

***

They reach the Waters of Nun. Amesemi and Bydos scamper down the sheer cliff toward the water's edge below.

"I'll wait here," Apedemak says, standing at the edge of a cliff overlooking the beach.

It's about one hundred yards down, but they've traversed this terrain since they could run free on their own. Today is no different. Bydos and Amesemi bound down the cliff with incredible speed.

They reach the shoreline and wait for Nun's onyx disc to

arrive.

Even at a distance from Nun's barge, Rah can see the others, and it puzzles him. *Speed suggests panic, and yet the others moved with purpose and discipline. They didn't seem to be afraid, but still...*

"Something is wrong," he calls out from behind Nun.

"It appears that way," Nun says as he closes his eyes and urges the vessel to gather pace.

"What do you suppose his response will be?" Bydos asks Amesemi, digging his foot into the cool, moist sand.

"That depends," Amesemi responds, "on just what caused all this calamity. Whatever happened, everything is different now. Your guess is as good as mine."

Bydos picks up a rock and launches it. It skips across the water for some way. Then a wave reaches up, catching it. The two of them are used to the waters behaving intelligently. They don't even flinch in response.

"Maybe we waited too late. Perhaps we should have asked sooner, before the earthquakes," Bydos says, digging into the soft sand with a spear.

Amesemi stares out toward Nun's ship. She dares not utter what she thinks for fear of scaring the boy.

Could Nun be the cause? Was this a form of retribution in exchange for Rah asking for his blessing?

As the vessel reaches the shallows, Amesemi stands and gathers her nerves.

An impatient Rah jumps from the disc as it glides into the shallows. He wades toward the shore, gliding through the dense current with ease. Amesemi and Bydos wait with bated breath.

He reaches the shore, his breath heavy more from concern than physical exertion. As he rises from the water,

Amesemi and Bydos run toward him.

"What is wrong? Do the earthquakes trouble you?" Rah asks as he rises from the water and walks ashore.

Bydos shakes his head. "It's Gilgamesh. He's gone."

Rah studies them, perplexed. "Gilgamesh is always gone. What's the worry?"

"He disappeared this morning, and now the land is rent asunder," Amesemi says. Her eyes dart to the shore as Nun's barge lands.

"That is why I returned with Nun," Rah says. "Things have changed."

"What is that supposed to mean?" Amesemi asks. "What did he say?"

She doesn't give Rah time to respond before she darts toward Nun, her anxiety increasing with each step through the firm warmth of the sand.

"Master, is everything all right?" Amesemi asks as she stops in front of Nun.

Bydos follows and steps beside her. "What of the earthquakes?"

Nun does not step down from his vessel. "I will explain, but only once you find Gilgamesh."

How did he know?

Their collective thought dissipates as Rah moves up the beach toward the facility. He glances around, sensing motion on the cliffs overhead.

Apedemak leaps from the cliff, landing in the trees.

This fool and his dramatics.

Rah shakes his head. It's really nothing personal; the two men are just wired differently. Apedemak considers things from an emotional level. He's quite intuitive. Rah, on the other hand, sees such emotions as proof of Apedemak's weakness. To him, the ability to silence one's emotions is the essence of strength. In his eyes, Apedemak's caving to emotions is akin to one cowering from a slap in the face, tears streaming down.

Physical strength alone will not ensure success. One must be both mentally and emotionally strong. These are the hallmarks of a ruler.

Within moments, Apedemak emerges from the trees. He nods in respect to Nun, then walks directly up to Rah.

"I see you've taken up Gilgamesh's knack for dramatic entrances in his absence," Rah scoffs.

"We were merely waiting for your return before going after him," Apedemak retorts.

Rah's confusion morphs into anger. "For what reason? Let the wild man run off as he always does. He will return."

"Not this time," Apedemak says, the look on his face silencing Rah. "Something is wrong; I can feel it. We warned him earlier to not run off, but as usual, he wouldn't listen."

Rah shakes his head in disbelief, then stares Apedemak dead in the eye. "Excellent leadership. All you have to do is control the situation for *one day* in my absence...but I know— you're the more capable leader, right?"

"I can track him," Apedemak says, circumventing Rah's trap. "If you follow my lead." Apedemak looks at Rah's icy glare.

How dare you challenge my authority.

"*Follow* you? You couldn't lead a wave to the shore," Rah says as Apedemak bites his lip in growing frustration.

"I haven't the time to explain my methods to you," Apedemak says with a menacing look, "and you lack the skill to understand." With that, he turns and walks toward Nun.

Rah, clenches his fists. "I will not be challenged," he says.

It happens before anyone senses it, even Nun. Apedemak turns around, and in a flash, Rah closes the distance, landing a crushing blow to his face. The blow catches Apedemak off guard. He and Rah haven't faced off in years; he wasn't expecting this.

Apedemak flies into a nearby boulder, cracking its surface. He lands in a heap. In his eyes lie a newfound respect for Rah, who stands before him unmoved as Apedemak regains his composure.

"Stay down," Rah warns.

Apedemak brushes his face before slowly rising to his feet. "My turn," he growls at Rah as he assumes a fighting stance and paces toward him.

Nun unleashes a roar that shakes the Earth. "Enough!" he yells. "This is neither the time nor the place for your petty squabbles! Rah will lead the search, and Apedemak will track him. Amesemi, you will accompany them." He turns to Bydos. "Bydos will remain with me to protect the facility."

Bydos looks at him, incredulous. "Why must I be the only one to stay?"

"It is not your time," Nun says. "Not yet."

Bydos doesn't care for this. He folds his arms and slouches, but out of respect, he says nothing more.

Nun turns toward the others. "You must go now. Bring him back—quickly. And refrain from further bickering. There are much more important issues at hand."

Rah turns to Apedemak and Amesemi. "Grab your gear," he says. "We leave immediately."

7 HORRORS OF THE PAST

Gilgamesh lies at the bottom of a deep chasm. He's been here for hours, maybe half a day since the earthquakes shook the Rift. The air in here is cold, moldy—the sheer walls jagged and damp.

He looks up, trying to gauge just how far he fell. It was long enough for his shock to morph into excitement, then wonder—*just how far is this drop?* he wondered as he clawed unsuccessfully for the walls around him. His wonder finally turned to fear as the gorge expanded into a vast vacuum of nothingness with no seeming end.

The impact was not pleasant, even compared to his normal bang-ups. He's reminded of this once more as he coughs and pain ruptures from his side. He probes his obliques and winces. *It seems I've broken more than one rib.* He coughs and wonders if it's blood he tastes at the back of his throat. His eyes dart, sensing sudden movement around him.

All along the rock face, glowing insects crawl in and out of unseen crevices, illuminating the space.

Again he looks up, pondering if he should attempt a climb toward the exit. A tiny sliver of light marks the surface above. The jagged rock face looms over him. Obsidian—one of Nun's favorite building materials. *Interesting.*

Still, the rock is much too sharp to climb, even for him. It's a wonder he didn't rip himself to shreds as he fell. *No way I can make it up there in this condition without risking another fall.*

Gilgamesh sighs. "How in the underworld do I get out of here?" He looks around, toward the deeper recesses of the cavern, and tries to coax himself back into good spirits. He forces a smile. "Quite an adventure, this is," he says, his voice trailing off slightly. "Even battered and bruised..."

Resolving himself to his circumstances, he begins an arduous trek into the cave, his usual swift gait now reduced to a halfhearted stagger.

He totters through the cave and immediately notices strange markings along the wall—deep engravings, easy to miss if it weren't for the insects nestling into their grooves, illuminating them. They're too precise, too regular to be anything natural.

"Is that writing?" Gilgamesh asks himself as he studies the markings. *It doesn't seem to be any alphabet I've ever seen.*

He continues further along, noticing even more markings. He rubs his fingers along them, careful not to cut himself as he peers at the tiny, ant-like insects scurrying about through the engravings.

"This was no accident," he says in stunned realization. He stops in his tracks and looks around. A sense of wonderment slowly morphs into concern—the kind that forms knots in throats and makes hairs stand up on-end. *What is this place?*

He travels quite a distance in the darkness searching for answers, stopping along the way to nurse the pain in his ribs until it slowly begins to subside. It's as if the insects purposefully guide him, lighting the way before him while rendering the cave behind him a void of trodden footsteps lost to the darkness.

As he stumbles forward, unsure of his destination, the air becomes moist. The rock dampens beneath his feet. In the distance he hears the faint trickle of water. The farther he traverses, water begins to trickle from the ceiling above him.

He wipes a drop from his forehead and rubs it between

his fingers. It's different from the Waters of Nun above, less dense. The spongy droplet bounces from his finger before he can grab it.

Suddenly, he reaches the end of the luminescent insect trail, takes one step beyond, and enters a large cavern. Though he can't see just how big it is, he feels the subtle brush of wind that alludes to the openness before him. The sound of liquid continues to build, so he follows it, stopping once his toes feel water.

The complete darkness makes his eyes work to produce a visual. He strains, and after a few moments, he can glimpse the edges of a subterranean lake. It gurgles as a water table farther below bubbles up, filling it with ripples that dance in the darkness.

He wonders if it's drinkable. A finger to his lips confirms that it is. Parched, he drops to his knees and gulps handfuls of water so greedily that he fails to notice he's not alone.

Just over his right shoulder, a bear snuffles through the cavern, its massive body now old and slow, its fur gone pale from a lack of sunlight. Nevertheless, it's still imposing as it passes, curiously eyeing Gilgamesh, though not seeming to mind his presence.

Gilgamesh grins warily at it. "Merely a traveler passing through, my friend. If you'll just let me clean my wounds in peace…"

He tends to his cuts and attempts to bind his ribs with a torn piece of his once-prized Sumerian robe.

The ground trembles, giving him pause. "Aftershocks?" Gilgamesh questions aloud.

No.

He quickly realizes that this is a regular pounding. Rhythmic. *Something else is coming. Something huge.*

"Time we were on our way," he says to the bear as he wearily stands, sporting a nervous grin.

The bear growls at him, standing his ground.

"Very well, then. It's been a pleasure," Gilgamesh says, looking around for an escape.

He could simply go back the direction he came. But the tunnel—with its low walls that lead to a dead end, coupled with his wounds—would render that a slow, arduous death march. He decides that his best bet is up, so he hobbles over to the nearest wall. Though he's not sure what kind of rock it is, he knows it's not obsidian. *This* he can climb. But the first extension of his arm upward sends pain coursing through his side.

More footsteps, closer this time.

Gilgamesh winces through his pain as he slowly wills himself up the trembling walls of the cavern—a handhold here, a foothold there. He scans his brain, searching for a thought to hold on to, anything to take his mind off of the agony plaguing his torso.

More footsteps, much closer.

Unsure of exactly what nears, Gilgamesh realizes that hanging out in the open sixty feet above ground isn't the most ideal place to be discovered. He looks around for another means of escape, or at least concealment.

He ascends a few more yards, and in the distance, he spots a dark shadow within the rock face. A recess has been carved into the wall just feet to his right and upward maybe another two yards.

More footsteps—too close for comfort this time.

The pain in his ribcage is almost unbearable as Gilgamesh pulls himself onto the ledge. He sits, but this causes sharper spikes of pain, so he opts to lie down, removing the stress from his ribs. The footsteps continue, causing the walls to shake more with each step. A few pebbles dislodge from overhead. A speck of dirt lands in his eye.

"Damn!" he shrieks reflexively as he struggles to remove the grain from his eye. He blinks and peers over the edge of the ledge down toward the water.

He can hear breathing now. Slow, deep breaths in-between footsteps. It's unlike any breathing pattern he's ever heard—deep breaths followed by a reticulating click.

What the underworld?

As the creature enters the cavern, Gilgamesh cranes his neck to get a better view. He's careful, however, not to alert the potential enemy to his presence.

Down below, the bear spots the intruder. It growls, backing up slowly.

"So this *is* a threat, then," Gilgamesh mumbles to himself, fully engaged in the scene unfolding below.

The bear swats the ground with its front paws and pops its jaws. Gilgamesh reads its behavior, sensing its fear. *Bears only respond like this when they're cornered, when they fear a fight. But what is it afraid of?*

It doesn't take long for his answer to arrive in the form of a horrid, alien clicking sound that resonates through the cavern.

"What *is* this thing?" he wonders aloud.

The bear rises onto its hind legs. It roars with a deep, full-throated bellow, ready to attack.

From the darkness, a serrated claw whips forward, crushing the unfortunate bear in its grasp. From Gilgamesh's vantage point, he can't make out much more than the fact that the creature's limbs appear to be long and crystalline.

The bear howls and claws in an attempt to free itself. Gilgamesh can hear the scrape of the claws against the creature's arm. It's a searing screech, the kind of scratching that makes your teeth grate. *That thing is rock. What the—*

The bear's claws seem to have no effect whatsoever on the creature. Its struggles only weaken it further as the massive claw tightens, slowly crushing the bear.

The creature moves forward. Gilgamesh can see it now—a mantis of some sort. Taller than a grown man, seemingly crafted from something other than mere flesh. Its inner core glows a bright red as its chest rises and falls with each breath. It would be almost beautiful if it weren't splattered with the life and blood from the bear in its grasp.

Gilgamesh recoils in shock at the sound of cracking bones as the bear lets out one last yelp of life. Gilgamesh thrusts himself backward toward the high wall behind him. A rock tumbles from the depression where he lies hidden and bounces to the floor of the cavern. *Damn!*

Gilgamesh lies still with sweat beads on his face. In his mind race a barrage of thoughts. *Did the creature hear the rock fall? Perhaps not. What is it? A demon? Alien?*

Down below, the creature looks at the bear's limp body and opens its mouth wide. Gilgamesh can't turn away from the sight, expecting the bear to be devoured.

Then he notices that the creature isn't exactly feeding—at least not on the flesh of the bear. Instead, it draws something from the corpse. Some bright and shining ethereal substance rips from the bear. "The soul," Gilgamesh whispers in wonderment.

Its work done, the creature tosses the limp bear into the lake, almost casually. Gilgamesh watches intently, sensing the worst is over.

Then the creature's deep red eyes glance toward Gilgamesh's hiding place. Through the darkness, its gaze fixes on him, lingering long enough to make Gilgamesh wish he'd listened to Apedemak and Amesemi for once and stayed in familiar territory.

In terror, Gilgamesh ponders meeting the same fate as the bear. He envisions himself within the creature's grasp, nervously babbling as he attempts to free himself to no avail.

Shaking such thoughts, he presses into the wall as much as possible, but this offers no camouflage. He resigns himself to his fate and musters up the courage to fight, refusing to go out as easily as the bear.

But after a tense moment, the creature turns to leave. It seems like an eternal trek. Still, Gilgamesh doesn't dare move until the heavy rumble of the cavern beneath the beast's feet is reduced to a memory.

He lies on his back, gazing downward toward the bubbling lake. In the darkness, the lifeless corpse of the bear drifts aimlessly, contaminating the waters that continually spring from some yet-unknown source.

Gilgamesh sighs in relief. He's safe, for now—as safe as anyone can be trapped underground in this hellish place. He begins to ponder his next adventure: the journey downward.

8 HOMELAND?

The Trail Is Hot—Rah's Personal Journal

So, this is where our training begins—with an unexpected crisis. Gilgamesh's trail leads toward the mountains. And so we follow, if somewhat slowly in the face of a world still changing by the hour.

The fool had **better** still be alive...If only so I can render necessary justice unto him for forcing us to rush into action unprepared. Only his screams begging for mercy at my hands could quell my current rage at his insolence.

***

Apedemak leads Rah and Amesemi on a cautious trek through the Flats, or what *should* be the Flats. The Upheaval would be a much more fitting moniker for this broken terrain that is now anything but flat.

Apedemak steps carefully through the area that for so long was their training ground. The massive earthquake split the land into thousands of fractured pieces, like those that form on ice just before it breaks.

Where great plains once stretched toward the horizon, now massive conglomerate of breccia stones jut skyward in natural monuments almost as tall as Apedemak himself. They create a jagged, uneven terrain that takes some skill to cross.

Amesemi shakes her head in horror. "But how could all this have—"

"The old man," Rah says.

Amesemi doesn't want to believe him, but then, Nun

didn't seem to be himself when he returned with Rah. And Rah had been right about the earthquakes. Then another thought causes her to pause.

Gilgamesh!

They cross another jagged slab of earth.

"He broke one of his crystals, said it was all a test for us," Rah continues.

Amesemi shakes her head. "It makes no sense. A test for what? Just what *happened* when you spoke to him, Rah?"

They approach the great lake.

"Stay alert. We must be cautious," Apedemak advises with a raise of his hand. "There are too many unknown factors out here for us to charge ahead."

The lake itself has also transformed. Large sections of the rocky plateau have broken off and crashed into the its thick waters. What was once a peaceful counterclockwise ebb and flow of gentle waves now courses at a rapid pace. Strange ruins break the surface as the water rushes around them.

Rah looks down at the sight below. Amesemi catches up to him and grabs his shoulder to get his attention. "What happened in the laboratory? What crystal? Tell me!"

"He called it a 'stabilization crystal,'" Rah says, his eyes still fixated on the torrential lake.

Amesemi's mouth wavers, searching for words. "That— that's—"

Apedemak places his hands on Rah's shoulders, stares him dead in the eye, and says, "Tell us exactly what happened with Nun."

Rah's eyes dart to Apedemak's hand. "I suggest you remove yourself."

Apedemak removes his hands but does not back down. "Did *you* cause this?" His finger sweeps toward the mountains in the distance that are wreathed in smoke. Magma streams down the upper slopes of several of the peaks. Farther away, the faint crackle of thousands of degrees of heat melting all in its path can be heard. Rah stares at the cataclysm.

Secrets!

Rah turns toward Apedemak, shrugging his shoulders in feigned nonchalance. "Concentrate on the mission. I know little more than either of you. Once we find Gilgamesh, we can discuss the Rift. I'm certain he will be able to provide us with more options."

Rah walks off and looks at the apocalyptic scene, leaving Apedemak alone to weigh his options. Apedemak's eyes dart to Amesemi as he tries once more to finally get a read on her mind.

Gilgamesh.

He casts his eyes downward in angst. *Even with all of this going on, all she can think of is Gilgamesh!* He walks away and resumes his tracking.

Amesemi walks over to Rah with a look of disgust. "You did this. I don't know what; I don't know how. But Nun would never do this on his own. When we find out—"

"What?" Rah asks in jest. Amesemi again searches for the proper words. It isn't fear that gives her pause in moments like these. It's the sheer overwhelming force of her emotions that is not easily distilled into words.

"Exactly," Rah says with a smile. "You have little right to complain of *my* performance on a mission that you lacked the courage to undertake yourself."

With that, he walks away, leaving Amesemi to her thoughts. *His hubris will lead to our demise. Why would Nun destroy a stability crystal? He knows that's the only thing stopping us from—*

She tries to derail her train of thought before it can

proceed. Some horrors are too much to imagine. *Besides, Nun couldn't be so reckless…or could he?*

She follows behind the others, transfixed by the volcanic eruption continuing its steady flow of lava across the lake. She watches as the lava meets the dense waters, absorbing the unfamiliar sound of water evaporating on contact. It's simultaneously soothing and terrifying.

She vaults another jagged piece of earth. Up ahead, Apedemak raises a quiet hand, signaling them to stop. He stares at the ground; it slopes downward here. With a forward wave of his hand, the others slowly approach him.

Apedemak crouches down low, and the others instinctively do the same. Only a short distance beneath them, strange crystalline beasts wander across the plain. The herd of beasts looks up, sees the party, and instantly flees.

Rah studies these peculiar animals. "They are much faster than their large bodies would suggest."

"I've seen them before," Amesemi says in shock.

Apedemak looks on in curiosity. "Where?" he asks.

Amesemi bites her tongue, unsure of how much of the laboratory's inner workings she is allowed to reveal to the others. Nun has always remained terribly secretive about his works.

"What hole could they have possibly crawled out of?" Apedemak asks no one in particular.

Rah gestures for the others to stand. He scans the horizon. "This is taking too long." He turns to Apedemak. "Can you still track him if we quicken the pace?"

"Simple enough at this stage," Apedemak replies as he points to the shore. Fresh hoof prints dot the moist sand below. "Our brother's horse," Apedemak continues. "I see no sign he abandoned it. Find his mount, and we find him.

Of this I am certain."

They scamper down the incline toward the shore. As they reach the sandy beach, Amesemi calls out, "I cannot run for miles at the speeds you two can manage."

Rah looks at her in annoyance. "You have not yet tried, sister."

"I could carry you on my back," Apedemak offers.

Rah turns toward the direction of the tracks, trying to get a read on where they could be heading.

Amesemi considers Apedemak's offer for a moment, then responds, "I would rather not burden you."

"You? A burden? Never," he says with a wry smile.

Amesemi is resolved. "Thank you, but no," she says with a smile. She stretches languidly in the sand. Apedemak quickly turns his head and studies the tracks. He feigns nonchalance, then heads off at a hunter's patient jog. Amesemi follows.

Rah shakes his head. *Can he make it any more obvious? He postures when I give a simple order, and yet one glance from that woman leaves him defenseless.*

Shaking the thought from his mind, Rah bursts into a sprint, his headdress blowing beside his ears as he catches up to the others.

***

After travelling for some time, they find Fadesh, Gilgamesh's horse, standing nervously on what appears to be a low hill. As they approach the animal, they notice a great chasm in the ground just on the other side. Smoke belches from below.

The horse yawns continuously. Rah turns toward Amesemi. "What's it doing?"

Apedemak approaches the horse cautiously. "He's slightly nervous, but there should be nothing to fear." He waves the others closer. "Come."

They move toward Fadesh. The animal gives them a wary glance, but its attention is otherwise fixed on the chasm. He neighs and lifts his head.

Amesemi approaches the horse and gently rubs its neck. "Is that where he went?" she asks, staring into the chasm.

Apedemak walks up beside her. "More than likely," he answers. "But is that where he meant to go?"

Rah steps to the edge of the crevice, studying its depth. "No matter," he says, looking at Apedemak. "We have to retrieve him, either way. Let's get down there."

Apedemak seizes the horse's mane and stares it in the face. A brief pause passes, and then the horse almost appears to nod. Apedemak releases his hand, and Fadesh bolts toward the flatlands from whence they came.

Amesemi looks at Apedemak with curiosity. "What was that? What did you just do?"

"I merely told him to return home," Apedemak responds, "and to be quick about it."

Amesemi smiles in amusement.

"Explain," Rah says as he steps toward Apedemak, who stares into the abyss.

"As I told you, I haven't the time to explain my methods." Apedemak turns his attention from the chasm to Rah. "And you lack the skill to understand."

Rah clenches his fists in anger but lets the impudence pass as Apedemak suddenly leaps into the chasm without hesitation.

9 FIND GILGAMESH

Apedemak drops deep into the crevice with barely a hint of effort. He lands flawlessly in a thick cloud of dust. His cough resonates deep within the chamber as he waits for the dust to settle and then surveys the surrounding darkness. Only once he's satisfied that the way is clear does he cup his hands and tilt his head skyward.

"It is safe to follow!" his voice bellows.

Rah descends slowly, climbing down the rock face. He grimaces as the obsidian begins to cut into his hands. Having traveled a few yards, he looks up with no sight of Amesemi.

"Time is of the essence, woman!" he yells.

From above, Amesemi looks into the darkness below. She questions the hasty decision of the others.

Apedemak shouts from below, "Perhaps it's best that we not call attention to ourselves."

Amesemi, on her hands and knees, leans over the edge above. She flinches as she gets a sense of the true depth of the opening. "We don't know what could be down there," she says.

"The rock is too sharp. You'll have to jump. Be expeditious. We don't have long," Rah says in annoyance.

Amesmi's face blanches at the thought. "Jump? Are you insane?"

From below, Apedemak forsakes his own advice to remain quiet. "I'll catch you," he says. "Trust me."

Rah continues his descent, quickly becoming annoyed at this tête–à–tête. *Perhaps the old man didn't mean it quite like this. Yet I see no other way.*

He looks up and sees Amesemi's hesitation and then strikes the wall in front of him. Though he uses a mere fraction of his power, the blow still cracks the rock wall. Shards of obsidian blast toward Rah's face as he too plummets into the hole, shielding his eyes.

The edge of the chasm where Amesemi crouches shudders, then breaks. She slips, and with a scream, she falls into the chasm.

Apedemak darts across the cavern, past the falling rocks and Rah, as he watches Amesemi bounce off of the wall and plummet toward him. Amesemi unleashes a stifling yelp just as she's about to hit the ground. She closes her eyes, bracing for impact.

She lands in strong arms that give under her weight and then sit her down gently.

Amesemi opens her eyes and shudders, unable to believe what just happened. She looks up and finds Apedemak staring at Rah with a burning fire in his eyes. He looks down at Amesemi quickly as he sets her down.

Uncomfortable with such vulnerability, she punches Apedemak square in his chest. She stands and dusts herself off, then spins around and yells at Rah, who wipes the blood from his hands onto his pants.

"I could have died!" she yells.

Rah studies his cuts as he strides deeper into the cavern, too unconcerned to even look in her direction. "Nun instructed me to trust the rest of you, and I did. I was certain he would catch you without fail."

For Amesemi, this seems to be enough. She shrugs and notices the cuts on her shoulder from tumbling into the wall. Apedemak walks over, tears off a piece of his loincloth, and without a word, wraps Amesemi's wound. She wants to thank him—she's almost certain that she does—but shakes the thought.

As Apedemak proceeds deeper into the cavern behind Rah, she lets the distance between them grow before she allows herself the freedom of further thought. *He acts with honor and guides with humility, and his thoughts are just and true. If we ever make it out of here, I'll...*

Her thought derails at the junction of reality and indecision. She continues forward, vowing to face that decision when—no, *if*—the time comes.

Up ahead, Apedemak jogs to catch up with Rah. He reaches him and nudges him with his shoulder. "You could have killed her with your recklessness!"

"But I didn't." Rah shrugs in nonchalance.

Apedemak grabs Rah's arm to stop him. "You will not do that again!"

Rah looks at Apedemak and smirks. "Or what, exactly?"

"There are untapped reserves of strength within me that I keep locked away out of respect for you as my brother," Apedemak says. "But should you place Amesemi in any danger again, the true nature of my unbridled fury will be revealed to you."

Rah finds Apedemak's display of bravado quite amusing as they enter a pitch-black portion of the cavern. Here, they pause momentarily, letting their eyes adjust to the dim light cast by the glowing insects.

Amesemi catches up to them and stops. "What are those strange, green glowing markings along the walls?"

Apedemak pauses and scans the dim surroundings. "He's here. Or he was," he says. "I can sense he passed this way. Let's go." Apedemak continues deeper with Amesemi on his heels.

Rah doesn't move. He stares intently at the markings along the wall. "A moment," he says as he crouches down to decipher the foreign language. "Only the Soulless may enter. The living must pass through like the wind. Keep to the hollow steps," he reads with a puzzled expression.

Apedemak stops to turn toward Rah, who scratches his head in confusion. He takes a few steps over to get a better sight of what Rah just read.

"And what could that mean?" Rah wonders aloud as Amesemi also approaches.

Apedemak looks down at Rah, who remains crouched. He can hardly contain his surprise. "You can read it?"

Rah looks up at him. "Is that so strange? You can't."

Amesemi walks up behind Rah, tracing her fingers along the strange letters. "After studying with Nun, I learned many languages," she says, "Yet it would still take a considerable amount of time to decode such a difficult text. Where did you learn this language? What is it?"

Rah continues to study the text, "I did not *learn* it. I simply looked and understood."

"Say that again?" Amesemi is perplexed.

Rah merely gives her an irritated look. Off to the side, Apedemak stares at the two of them, visibly puzzled.

Amesemi's eyes light up in realization. "This is Cuneiform! The Anunnaki favored this style of writing and taught it to the locals in Sumer. The language is more refined now. This is a particularly archaic script—very old."

"I thought you couldn't read it," Rah says, looking at Amesemi in annoyance.

Amesemi shakes her head. "I can't. But I have seen it before, during my studies with Nun."

"How would you interpret this text, then? 'Only the

soulless may enter. The living must pass through like the wind. Keep to the hollow steps,'" Rah asks.

Amesemi kneels down beside him. "The Anunnaki favored what were known as conditional sanctuaries—rules laid down in the very heart of the things they built, not unlike a curse upon the very stone itself. We should tread carefully. Let nothing out of the ordinary pass without notice."

"Very well." Apedemak says as he turns and resumes his trek. Amesemi rises and presses deeper into the cavern along with him.

Rah remains a few steps behind them, pondering upon the inscriptions on the wall.

Soulless?

Soon, they find themselves engulfed in an ocean of darkness, the sky itself no more than a memory.

"It's like a prison," Amesemi remarks as the walls become tighter.

"Indeed!" Rah bellows from behind her and Apedemak, his mind continuing to wander. *And should our luck take a turn for the worse, we will have little hope of escape.*

He pulls out a papyrus scroll and a small pen from his loincloth and scrawls in the darkness.

Down into the Darkness—Rah's Personal Journal

So, this is where Gilgamesh has run off to—some hidden place beneath the old man's broken kingdom. We descended into the depths of the earth without incident.

Apedemak and Amesemi are still chattering. It is quite annoying...I hope these two cease their endless banter soon. This is a time to be alert. There are secrets down here that hint at just how unknown the Rift truly is. I sense great danger within these tunnels...

10 SOULLESS

After travelling for some distance into the cave, they reach a junction where the path through the rock forks in multiple directions.

Ever cautious, Amesemi warns them, "We should stick together. This place is not…natural."

"But if we split up, we may find him faster," Apedemak says.

Amesemi turns to him, surprised by his differing opinion. His protective presence is one she'd assumed she could count on during such an arduous trek. Now the thought of exploring this underground labyrinth alone sends shockwaves of fear rippling through her.

As if sensing her apprehension, Apedemak explains, "If the tunnels seem to be leading us nowhere, we can always return to this location."

"I agree," says Rah. "Nothing we have found so far has posed any danger to us. We should split up. Time is of the essence."

With that, Apedemak draws a javelin from the sheath on his back. "Then it's decided. I'll take the middle passage," he says, placing a concerned hand on Amesemi's shoulder. "Don't worry. I can sense you through the rock. Should you run into any trouble, I can find you."

"A good plan," Rah says with a nod.

Outnumbered, Amesemi knows putting up an argument is of no use. "If you insist…" she acquiesces.

Rah heads toward the rightmost tunnel. He turns suddenly, looking from Amesemi to Apedemak. "Remain cautious, both of you." He tries to conceal the concern in his voice. "We may not have encountered any obstacles thus far, but this is no guarantee the way ahead will be clear."

Amesemi moves into the leftmost tunnel, where the ground slopes downward. Apedemak watches her enter. He hesitates a moment, then steps lightly into the tunnel straight ahead.

***

The minutes that pass feel like days gone by. Traversing deeper into the chamber, Amesemi's only companion is the thoughts in her mind. *The air is cool, moist. That smell…*

"Is that water?" she wonders aloud to herself. But there is something else there—another darker scent, she's certain. She stops, not wanting to proceed further until she can be certain. Amesemi raises her hands before her:

> Spirits of the Ancients, I ask of thee,
> Find favor with mine call and summons.
> On the four winds, I beg thee travel,
> And greet me in mine presence.
> Khamaseen winds, thy powers do I wish to invoke.
> Come now;
> So shall it be.

Slowly, a light breeze forms and wafts toward her from the other end of the tunnel with a slight wave of her hand. She almost gags as the stench reaches her.

Blood.

She continues on, trying to quiet the fear raging in her mind. *Please don't let it be Gilgamesh. Oh, why did he run off? The feeling I had—I should have known.*

83

Her thoughts finally cease as she turns a corner and spies a subterranean lake. The water glows with a subtle fluorescent shimmer.

She scans the surface for the source of the blood and spots a carcass in the shallows. Her heart drops as she continues closer, entering the cavern.

"Gilgamesh," she whispers faintly as she approaches the edge of the water. She crooks her neck sideways, wondering if she's seeing things. "Unusual," she whispers.

She approaches slowly, her narrowed eyes scanning the surface. A red cloud hangs motionless in the water with crimson tendrils winding across the surface.

Blood.

She strains to focus through the darkness at the object floating in the lake. It's an animal of some sort—a large one. The corpse has been horribly mutilated beyond recognition, almost crushed. Her elation in the realization that it's not Gilgamesh is quickly cut short as she imagines the danger lurking around her. *What could have done this?*

A strange noise echoes through the cave. The air itself warps and twists, like a regular hissing pulse at the edge of her hearing.

Amesemi trembles, then the ground responds in kind, as if it senses her fear. Something is drawing closer. She scans the cave around her. Finding nowhere she might hide, she decides it's better to stand her ground than flee.

She kneels down, dips her cupped hands into the water, then slowly raises them as she chants.

"El maa adad!"

The water from the lake rises at Amesemi's accord, following her hands. It climbs in a wobbling pillar; then, as Amesemi shifts, the churning column of liquid begins to encircle her. A current forms around her, creating a knee-deep a whirlpool.

Suddenly, a pebble clips her in the side of the head. "Ow!" She nearly loses control of the water as her focus shifts.

"Over here," a voice whispers harshly.

She recognizes the voice. "Gilgamesh?"

Amesemi lets the enchantment go. Immediately, the water falls back into the lake, splattering everywhere. Amesemi pays no mind as her eyes seek familiarity in the foreboding darkness.

There he is! Gilgamesh.

Only a short distance away, huddled in a shallow depression in the ground, Amesemi spots the reflection of those mischievous eyes. She rushes over and looks down upon him. "How did you—"

"Quiet!" Gilgamesh whispers hurriedly. "Get down here. Move!"

Too surprised to question the order, Amesemi climbs into the hole. With a muttered curse and a grunt of effort, Gilgamesh reaches out for an immense boulder and hauls it back into place over their hideaway, leaving just enough of a gap so they can see up into the cave.

Amesemi whispers in the darkness, "What are we—"

"Shh," Gilgamesh urges. "Keep quiet. This *isn't* the time for an interrogation."

There's no sign of the creature, but Amesemi can feel the increasing reverberations through the ground as the beast marches into the cavern. The noise increases until it becomes a deafening pounding.

Then, it stops.

They close their eyes in fear—neither of them need a

visual to determine that the creature is directly above them. Its ferocious breathing and resulting articulated click sends ice coursing through Amesemi's veins.

She slowly opens her eyes and can only catch brief glimpses of the creature as it shifts its weight above, studying the boulder. But what she sees is enough to cause her to question everything she's known. The creature is huge—two or even three times the height of a man—only it's nothing remotely human.

A pale light reflects off of a hard, glittering, rocklike skin—black marble, perhaps—wreathed in tendrils of dark smoke that seep from its unseen pores. Her heart rate increases. *And I planned on fighting this thing?*

She dares not utter a word; it's hard enough to breathe. Beside her, Gilgamesh is a warm presence, though he too holds his breath, unable to move.

I'm surprised he cared enough to not let me walk right into its claws.

Her thoughts are quickly interrupted by a strange, distorted sound coming from the creature. It's intense. She and Gilgamesh jam their hands against their ears in reaction.

Suddenly, another louder noise crackles from overhead. It's a deep, guttural roar that sounds like rocks grinding together, tortuously—slowly. The sound stutters in a regular rhythm as if produced by magic of some unknown sort. *Is that speech?* If it is, then it doesn't resemble any language she knows.

The cavern around them trembles, but this time it's not the creature. Something else has moved deep within the earth. Through the slit in the rock obscuring them, she sees the creature swing around—the sudden, unmistakable reaction of a predator sniffing the air. Without warning, the creature charges off, the ground shuddering with every hurried step.

For a long moment, they sit stunned in silence, wondering if the monstrous being is really gone. Then, without a word, Gilgamesh reaches up and heaves the rock aside.

Amesemi scrambles out of the hole and reaches down to help him out in turn.

"We have to get out of here," she says, her breathing frantic. "The others came to—"

"To find me," Gilgamesh beams, full of pride. He climbs up from the hole and dusts himself off. "Yes, of course they did. I *am* the most important, after all."

Amesemi frowns at his arrogance. "They were worried!"

"Worried? Why, I've handled myself quite well. Some of us have the stomach for adventure, and others...well," he pauses in thought. "Never mind. If that...*thing* finds them, they'll have something much more pressing to worry about."

He steps forward with a pronounced limp. Amesemi notices bruising on his ribs and leg.

"Can you walk?" she asks.

He takes another step and winces in pain. "Yes, but not very fast. I injured my ribs when the crevice opened up beneath me and I fell. My leg—scampering into that hole," he says. "Come. Give me your arm, or else we'll never find those two before that monster."

***

Apedemak climbs through the tunnel. Jagged rocks lie under his feet. Cool water trickles between his toes. The uneven terrain and winding path forces him to slow his pace until he finds himself at a dead end.

This can't be the end.

He feels around; the space is tight, not even wide enough for him to stretch out his arms. But overhead, the space expands. *There.*

He grabs onto the wall. The sharp obsidian digs into his flesh, causing him to rethink. He grabs another piece of his loincloth, rips it in two pieces, and wraps both of his hands. He reaches out for the walls again. *Better.* His uncovered fingertips will still bear the brunt of the torture, but it's a small price to pay.

He climbs straight upward, hand over hand, until he reaches the top of a huge slab of rock. He hurls himself up, grateful to give his fingertips a reprieve.

It's a narrow ledge, almost a wall, dividing two spaces. He surveys the scene; there's nowhere to go but down. Refusing to turn around, he uses all four limbs to slowly descend the narrow gap into the unknown.

What happened out there? To the Rift? What did Nun do…and why?"

His feet hit dry dirt. Immediately, the ground lights up as florescent-green insects scatter. He's reached the bottom, another narrow crevice through which he must navigate.

He proceeds forward through the dim light provided by the insects on the ground and low along the walls. There seem to be endless turns and forks within this labyrinth of rock, each one unlocking another thought within his mind.

Was it Rah? Something he said to Nun? I should have gone instead. He clenches his fists as he treks deeper into the unknown. *I could have convinced him. Nun would have listened to me.*

He visualizes Amesemi, alone in one of the lower tunnels, and questions her safety. For a moment he has to fight the impulse to rush back down and find her. *She can look after herself. But...I should be with her—just to make sure she's safe.*

He knows Rah doesn't understand their burgeoning connection. He's seen the other man's expression while watching the two of them talk. But then, how could he? Rah, by nature, seems to know no other emotion besides anger. Apedemak scoffs at Rah's disapproval. *As if he understands. As if he even has a heart.*

Apedemak scans his brain, attempting to recount a time when he's seen Rah crack a simple smile. He walks for a while and still can't seem to conjure such a memory.

In a way, Apedemak pities Rah. For all of his brute strength, he's too hardened to appreciate the simple joys of human existence—the morning sun and newness of day, the laughter or touch of a woman. No, all that brings Rah joy is destruction and violence. Apedemak shakes his head in disgust.

Though Nun would like for us to depart the Rift together, at the first opportunity I will separate myself and Amesemi from his destructive energies, lest they wreak havoc upon our destinies as well.

The tunnel rumbles slightly. Something massive passes through the cave complex a fair distance away.

Apedemak stops, crouches in the darkness, and reaches out to touch the ground. He lets his senses burrow through the rock, homing in on Rah and Amesemi's energies. *Hmmm. Neither of them seems to be in immediate danger. Very well.*

The tunnel stops up ahead. He can feel it.

He approaches a giant stone gateway, half-buried in the debris of cumbrous fallen rocks. Clearly people of some sort once passed through this tunnel. He can still see the thin gap between the walls. *If I could just open them.*

He tugs at the door to no avail. It's locked.

There are inscriptions in the stone. These characters are different from those at the entrance to the cavern. Apedemak moves closer, trying to make sense of the writing with the help of the light from the glowing insects.

It appears to be…Anunnaki script. But what does it say?

For perhaps the first time in his life, he wishes that Rah were by his side, if only to provide a translation.

***

Rah walks through a charnel house. The tunnel is dry and cold and littered with bones—old bones, white and brittle. These are the only remnants of bodies buried ages ago, some alien, and some animal.

He stops to pluck one or two from the floor, briefly examining them before tossing them aside. *No claw marks. No gashes made by tools. I see nothing to show what stripped away the flesh. So how did they die? Were they trapped inside?*

He remembers the initial warning on the cavern wall and frowns.

Soulless.

The passage climbs. This is no longer a random fissure through the rock. The tunnel has been hollowed out, purposefully widened. People, or some type of intelligent beings, created this space with intent. And now a wall stands across the path. It's not a mere barrier. This is the edge of some great structure that someone, or something, built down here. But the wall has been shattered, and the stones have split apart from floor to ceiling.

Could it have been the earthquake that did this when Nun broke the gem, or something else?

He squints to look through the cracks in the stone and

catches a slight glimpse into the ancient structure. He can't make out much more than shadows, but this is enough to sense a vast, empty space beyond the gap.

Rah remembers Nun's words of warning about strength in numbers, but in the moment, curiosity trumps cooperation. *Besides, Gilgamesh could be just on the other side.*

Rah continues searching for a rationale to proceed. *Surely nothing in there could be of too much danger.*

Once assured, he squeezes through the crack in the wall.

BANG!

Upon entrance into the vast space, he is stunned by a sudden blue flare followed by a hissing, crackling sound. Before he even has time to make it out, the bolt of lightning strikes Rah so hard he's instantly rendered unconscious.

Soulless.

The Rift.

Chaos.

Nun's mighty hand.

The crushing pain.

Apedemak and Amesemi.

Gilgamesh.

Gilgamesh!

Rah's eyes open to the darkness. *Where am—? The flash of light. What was that?*

Rah rolls over and pulls himself up onto his hands and knees. A throbbing pain shoots through his head.

"Things more powerful than you," a familiar voice says. Rah shakes his head, hoping to evict the voice as he stands.

Focus. Stay focused.

He staggers helplessly across the chamber, nauseated. He bumps into a wall and rests his body weight against it as he catches his breath.

Compose yourself!

As he comes to his senses, a wretched smell hits his nose. The air reeks of burnt flesh. His eyes scan the darkness, searching the shadows for the threat, yet there's nothing.

"Only the soulless," the voice in his head says again. He refuses to respond to the voice, fearing that will only encourage it further. *It's nothing. It's a figment of my imagination. I've made it this far. Whatever that was just caught me by surprise.*

Realizing that if it were something that wanted him dead, he would have been taken out while he lay there unconscious, he stifles a growing sense of panic.

After a few moments, his nausea wears off. He allows his fingertips to check his body for injury. The blow isn't severe; he's not gravely injured. His clothes are intact, and his head is already clear.

He looks up and around. *A defense mechanism of some kind—lightning striking out to ward off intruders.*

A sense of confidence surges through him. *If this is the most the ruins can manage, we should have Gilgamesh out of here in no time!*

Once again feeling sure of himself, Rah wanders deeper into the ancient halls. Apart from the earth creaking in the distance and a thin scuttling sound within the walls, all is quiet.

The same dim golden light from the caves outside has settled on the corridors. He scans the ceiling but can't find a potential light source. Still, from what he can observe, the cavern has the feeling of some ancient, sacred site.

He senses there's still danger lurking nearby. This place is huge, for one thing. He has no idea where Gilgamesh might be, or if he even came this way. *And…what are these deep, regular grooves in the stone?*

"Claw marks?" he questions aloud. There's a sound in the distance—a furious roar. The ruins around him tremble. Something very big and angry approaches.

I knew it!

"Damn!" Rah says, his head on the swivel, seeking an outlet. He could flee in the direction he came, but then he'd be running away across open ground with a very large threat hard on his heels.

That would be foolish.

There are doors in here, but from the runes he can decipher along the walls, going west would lead him further into the depths and straight into more potential calamity.

There!

He spots a smaller door on the wall adjacent to the narrow opening he squeezed through. It could give whatever's coming a harder time following him.

He sprints across the open space and reaches the door only to find that it has no handle. As he stands there pushing and pounding upon the door, he finds himself wishing he had an inkling of Amesemi's understanding of technology. *If she were here, she'd be able to get this thing open, no doubt.*

The rumbling draws nearer.

Nun's words echo through Rah's mind: "There were things trapped beneath this realm—beings of fearsome power that could overpower me, if given the chance."

Rah frantically brushes against the door, seeking some sort of manual release. *If those beings could overpower the old man, what fate could befall me...or the others?*

There it is!

A panel hangs over a recess in the wall! Rah strikes the cover with a judicious blow to knock it loose. He peers inside and notices a series of gears; the inner workings are strange but somewhat understandable.

The thing in the distance is getting closer.

Rah grabs an onyx pick from his bracer and begins to force the mechanism. His pick shatters in the process, but the door clatters to life. As it opens, Rah spots a figure on the other side.

It's Apedemak, who stares at him as if he's seen an apparition. He blinks, then finally finds his voice. "Rah? What are you—"

"No time," Rah says as he begins to climb through the rubble between the two of them. "We have to run."

Apedemak's eyes swell in surprise as he points behind Rah. "Gilgamesh?"

Rah turns to spot Gilgamesh and Amesemi staggering down an unseen embankment along the perimeter of the expanse, headed toward them. Gilgamesh has an arm around Amesemi's neck as she balances his weight.

"Run, you idiots!" Gilgamesh yells, "There's—"

His warning is drowned out by the crash of falling rocks, pebbles, and dust coupled with the creature's frenzied bellow.

Amesemi struggles to carry both herself and Gilgamesh while ducking debris.

Apedemak gathers his spears and throws them to Rah.

"I'll carry him," Apedemak barks over the resounding chaos. "Amesemi, come on. Rah can serve as the rear guard. He's the strongest—"

"Not enough to stand against that thing," Gilgamesh says as they reach Apedemak and Rah. Gilgamesh's voice is noticeably devoid of his usual playfulness. "No heroics, brother. Its power—"

He coughs. Blood stains his chin.

Rah studies Gilgamesh, then whips his head toward the

ever-increasing sound coming toward them. He looks at Apedemak, his face creased in seriousness. "I have no intention of dying tonight. Move out!"

Gilgamesh climbs unsteadily onto Apedemak's back, and they flee through the newly opened door. After a long pause, glancing back down the corridor into the ruins, Rah shoulders his brother's spears and follows at a distance.

11 RUN

Amesemi leads the way as she and Apedemak sprint through the narrow tunnels with Gilgamesh jolting up and down, clinging onto the warrior's back.

"Do you have any idea where we should be going?" Apedemak yells at Amesemi.

"I can sense the wind coming down each path. We must follow the fresh air. Here," she says, pointing to a bend in the tunnel up ahead, "this way!"

"Excellent. I'll mark the walls for Rah as he passes," Apedemak says, brandishing a knife as he runs. He strikes the rock as they pass, cutting deep grooves into the stone at every fork in the path to mark their route of escape.

Gilgamesh stirs weakly and looks behind him. "It's so faint. Will he even notice? What if he—"

"He'll be fine. He can handle himself," Apedemak says without so much as a backward glance.

"I'm afraid even Rah himself is no match for that thing one-on-one," Gilgamesh says with a cough.

Apedemak ponders if Gilgamesh could be correct. After all, he's never seen his brother gripped with such terror. Finding these thoughts too disconcerting, he casts them to the deeper recesses of his mind and charges forward. "He'll read the walls. He'll make it."

***

Much farther behind the others, Rah makes his way through the tunnel at just enough speed to stay out of the creature's reach. Though he realizes the immense danger he's placing himself in, a part of him wants to get a glimpse of this strange being—*needs* to get a glimpse of it. It could be an answer to one of Nun's riddles, after all. It could even reveal the truth behind his myriad secrets.

The markings on the wall reflect a faint glow. Many of them are sliced through. He studies them while running. *These weren't here before.*

His fingertips rub along the groove. The warmth he feels isn't from the tiny insects lurking within but from friction.

These grooves are fresh. They marked the way.

The pounding behind him continues unabated, a reminder to stay focused and not let his mind wander.

As the cave before him forks, the groove ends. Without looking further, Rah heads toward the left, ducking into another passage. He traverses a few yards deep into the tunnel, then stops. Too far ahead and he could lose the beast entirely. No, he must bear witness. After his failed challenge outside of the temple, defeating this creature could restore his image, both with himself and in the eyes of Nun.

The screeching of the creature's claws along the wall announces its arrival.

"Run," the voice says with a hiss.

He catches a glimpse of the creature as it rounds the corner. It bashes into the surrounding wall in an attempt to squeeze itself into the small corridor.

Even through the darkness, Rah can sense the creature's terrifying size. As it approaches the fork in the tunnel, it stops, looks left, and stares dead at Rah, who watches just yards deep into the tunnel. *How did it know to turn? Was it my scent? How intelligent is this monster?*

Rah's thoughts are interrupted as the creature bellows into the tunnel; its roar is deafening. Rah covers his ears, fighting off his growing sense of dizziness caused by the sound.

The voice inside his head yells this time—"Run!" But Rah is defiant.

Though the monster's bulk barely fits in the tunnel, it doesn't seem to care. It uses its hardened exterior to grind away at the softer rock wall, and it accomplishes its feat with remarkable speed. Once it manages to enter the tunnel, it charges in Rah's direction with lightning speed and unbelievable agility.

Rah takes off running, his only map a narrow green strip in an ocean of foreboding darkness.

The creature continues to bash its way through the narrow tunnel, thrusting its mass forward, splintering shards of rock until it reaches a wider portion of the tunnel where it can again move freely.

Rah sprints at a furious pace, now regretting his decision to tease the creature. He can only make out the directional markings intermittently now. Each time he loses sight of it, panic begins to dance through his body, and he wonders if he's lost. In these moments he develops a new appreciation for the others and their skill sets.

He admits to himself that perhaps Apedemak is correct, and his brute strength alone is not enough to survive. Then he realizes that he'd rather be crushed by the beast than to openly admit such a thing.

As he comes to another large crack in the wall, just large enough for him to slide through, he shakes the disconcerting thought from his mind. *The green groove ends here. They must have gone inside.*

Rah presses himself between the crack. He pauses momentarily and ponders. *Another lightning strike, or face whatever this creature is?*

Quickly surmising that he survived the first lightning strike, he decides to take his chance again as he climbs through the passage and finds himself once again in the large, cavernous charnel house. Somehow while attempting to follow the groove, he's lost his way.

We're running in circles? This is a death march. Surely this beast knows these caverns better than we.

He moves deeper into the interior of the space. He can hear the increasing rumble of the creature. Nearer it gets, then nearer still, until it comes to the door. It pauses there. Rah can hear its distinct, clicking inhales and exhales.

Is it too large to enter? Has it given up?

Rah keeps his eye on the entrance, his tension slowly abating. Then, the pounding begins.

Loud, thunderous pounding.

Rah scans for signs of the others, for another luminescent green groove—any means of escape. Finding none and realizing that more running will only diminish his strength further against this creature, he decides to stand his ground and fight.

Boom. Boom. Boom-boom!

The being continues to pound upon the entrance, finally smashing its way into the charnel house. It demolishes the surrounding wall in the process.

Old man, what have you set loose?

The creature crouches down to fit inside the space. As it enters, it stretches out to its full height and faces Rah. Twice his height or more, it's a hulking, demonic figure with vicious-looking horns and hollow eyes. Its long, narrow mouth is full of jagged teeth only to be outdone by its sharp and gigantic claws.

It stands before Rah, momentarily frozen—a statue of some nightmare that crawled out of the depths of the earth. But this is no statue. It's made of glittering black rock that heaves as the creature breathes intensely.

Rah's eyes fixate on the crimson fire boiling inside it. His mind attempts to fathom the black smoke billowing out of the joints where its body cracks and reforms. And in return, it is studying Rah. Yes, there's a distinct presence behind that empty gaze.

It seeks my doom.

Rah's hand slowly moves of its own will, instinctively snatching one of Apedemak's spears. He brings his arm back and hurls the spear with more force than he's ever mustered.

It's a good throw. Damn good. The spear flies true, striking the creature full in the chest. The sheer speed at which he launched it makes the creature reel backward upon impact.

He felt that.

Rah reloads, grabbing another spear in preparation to launch. But his growing confidence wanes as the creature swats at the spear, breaking it in half. The creature roars again, then takes two large steps toward Rah.

How? The blow had no effect?

He surmises that only something massive and heavy can truly injure the creature. While keeping his eyes on the monster, Rah pounds his hand into the wall to his left. It cracks and begins to splinter. The creature watches this with curiosity, its head tilting from side to side.

A gigantic slab of rock dislodges. Rah centers his strength and grabs the huge chunk of stone. He lifts it high above his head, then launches it at the creature. It strikes with a loud bang of stone against stone, knocking the creature down. Its limbs writhe as it lies immobile under the weight of the stone.

Brute strength isn't so overrated after all.

Rah turns and begins to scan for an exit passage.

Then the rustling begins.

He spins around and finds the creature's claws attempting to gain leverage on the rock. Its massive body rocks and shifts under the weight, and soon it manages to lift the rock off itself. Rah watches in horror as it casts the rock aside, steadies itself, and stands.

What the—

As the creature tilts its head back and screams in rage, Rah is forced to admit he has only one sensible option left to him.

He runs.

***

Rah runs faster than he has in years, perhaps ever! Having just ran this route, he knows exactly where to go.

He sprints through the tunnels with the creature hot on his tail. The close quarters keep it from gaining on him too much, but still, it's not the advantage he would like. As he again studies the marks along the walls, he concentrates his energy on contacting his brother.

Apedemak. If I know where I'm going, perhaps I can turn the tables.

An image jumps into his mind. His eyes dart to the right. There, yards away, he spots a junction in a blind corner. He'd missed it before when he split left the first time. With his energy rapidly depleting, to make the same mistake again could prove fatal.

He turns left across the junction and runs straight for the wall. He can feel the creature's heavy tread close behind him. Its claws continue to grasp for him, scratching along the wall in the process. It's a teeth-grating sound that makes the hair on Rah's body stand at attention.

No other chance. Now!

At the last moment, Rah sprints up the wall to his left and leaps outward. The creature roars as Rah vaults overhead, barely making it into the small opening in the wall to his right. He tears his skin on the rock as he lands, but it's a small price to pay. He hobbles down the new passage, keeping his head on the swivel to survey all that's behind him.

Just outside the passage, the creature's massive momentum sends it careening into the side of the tunnel, completely destroying the wall. It lies there momentarily, stunned. *That buys me…no more than a few moments. Still—it's all I need.*

Emboldened by his triumph, Rah picks up his pace and is already deep into the new tunnel. He continues at an unsteady gait and suddenly spots a familiar, faint groove along the wall.

They can't be far.

More pounding. Rah can only assume that the creature is again pounding his way through the passage's narrow inlet.

This thing will not relent.

He feels a burgeoning sense of trepidation as he rounds a corner, but to his surprise, he finds the others trudging through the tunnel at a jogger's pace.

Unaware of Rah gaining ground behind them, Amesemi gestures up ahead toward the end of the tunnel. "The outside air. We're almost there," she says.

Rah feels an intensifying heat upon his back. He turns to

see long black and red flames leaking from the creature's body and reaching through the tunnel toward him with gargantuan twisted claws.

Fire?

Amesemi turns around and catches a glimpse of the inferno raging toward them.

Rah turns and locks eyes with Amesemi. "Don't stop, you fools! Move!"

Exhausted, Amesemi screams toward Apedemak and Gilgamesh, who are slightly ahead of her. "We must move faster! It's gaining on us."

Rah turns to face the oncoming threat.

More time. I must buy a little more time.

The creature picks up speed, as if it knows its prey is on the verge of escape.

Rah thinks intently.

One last trick. Something—anything!

Then it comes to him. "Barriers," he says to himself with a smile.

With a grunt, Rah slams his fist into the surrounding walls, making one hole, then another. Each thrust of his fist sends large stones spewing out into the cavern, creating a field of debris. He stops and pounds repeatedly in one section until enough rock has fallen to completely obscure the path between him and the creature.

He repeats this process two more times deeper inside the cave until his hands, bloodied and raw, can take no more. His work done, he turns and runs, then stops to look back.

The monster claws through the walls of sediment, slowing down only slightly. It seems worth noting.

Can anything stop this thing?

Resigned to the fact that he has no defense against the

creature, Rah rushes to catch up to the others, who have quickened their pace.

The passage narrows considerably. It's much tighter now as they enter what may have originally been an air shaft. The creature can't seem to claw its way through the rock with such ease any longer. It hauls its way forward in violent lurches. The black smoke from its marbled limbs almost fills the tunnel.

Is it tiring?

He can't be sure, and it's not worth the risk to find out, so Rah presses forward.

Behind him, the creature howls and thrashes, straining to claw its way through the passage behind him. Rah can feel it—this burning, otherworldly desire to rend him into a thousand bloody pieces.

More fire.

Damn!

He can't revel just yet in the freedom of total escape. It's still too close. If just one of those searing claws reaches him…

Light?

Up ahead, he can clearly see the exit now—the welcoming salvation of dawn's light. But the long, fiery claw snakes through the tunnel closer…closer…its heat now beginning to burn the flesh on Rah's back.

Rah struggles through the pain as he nears the exit. He blinks at the daylight streaming down the passage and realizes the opening is far too small to allow the creature to follow them. He's almost there.

Almost…

At the last second, he notices, but it's far too late to stop the momentum propelling him forward. The light from the cavern falls into another deep gorge, a hole in the cavern floor. Rah lets out a yell as he plunges toward the cool waters below.

The force of the fall carries him deep underwater. He feels his way through the darkness, waiting for his eyes to adjust. Then, high above, a large flame erupts. The creature has reached the drop. The flames rain down onto the surface of the lake, casting all within Rah's line of vision with an eerie orange glow.

He scans, looking for an exit.

Could the others have come this way?

He swims farther, with sudden bursts of flames intermittently lighting his way. Each burst provides only a couple of seconds of light, and with his air running out, Rah knows he must act fast.

Then he spots it—a small hole in what appears to be a wall underneath the lake. Sunlight streams in from beyond.

High above, the creature pounds on the rock face, sending sharp fragments and large boulders plunging into the waters below. One hit and Rah could be killed. He doesn't doubt that. Experience reminds him that this thing will not relent until it's succeeded.

He swims toward the opening. Something floats toward him, narrow and dark. As it nears, he notices it—a piece of Apedemak's loincloth.

They did come this way!

Rah's resolve is strengthened as he reaches the opening. It's large enough for him to swim through without much effort. He pulls himself through to the other side and bolts upward.

He breaks the surface and gasps for air.

12 GRAVITY

Nun stands guard atop his boat as it idles at the edge of the lake, somewhere deep beneath the towering cliffs on the northwest side of the Rift. The great onyx disc rocks ever so slightly with the ebb and flow of the waves. He waits patiently for his kin to return, hopefully with their missing companion in tow.

Of course, Gilgamesh could be anywhere. But Nun has assessed the damage the earthquakes caused to the Rift. He knows where the young man is most likely to have gone seeking adventure. He could have told his kin the exact location, yes, but better they find out for themselves.

A flock of birds glides above a waterfall overhead, catching Nun's attention. As he watches, a cloud meanders in front of the sun. Such tranquility above juxtaposes the unknown but certain chaos below.

Then, a faint sound disturbs his reverie. A roar sounds somewhere way off but loud enough to work its way right through the rock. He feels a flicker of concern.

Loose stones tumble down the cliffside adjacent to the waterfall. There is a scream. Something, or someone, vaults from the waterfall. One, two, three, four.

Rah plunges into the water with a force that takes his breath away. For a moment everything is a whirlpool of bubbles. His pulse hammers in his ears as he rockets back upward to break the surface once more, gasping for air.

He is alive and unhurt, save for the slight burns on his back. It doesn't appear that the creature was able to make it out of the cavern. But if so, the rapids will bring it this direction swiftly. He looks around for others.

Amesemi pops up next to him, treading water and spluttering. "That was insane," she says between heaves as she replenishes her oxygen.

"At least we made it," Rah says, attempting to quell his nerves.

She brushes her wet hair back and slowly, grudgingly nods. "Are you all right?"

"It would appear so," Rah says as he quickly remembers the others. He spots Gilgamesh floating next to Apedemak, who has one arm keeping Gilgamesh's head above water. "Gilgamesh," he calls out. Gilgamesh is battered, and his eyes are closed, but his chest continues to rise and fall slowly with each breath.

"Out cold. The impact from the fall, I'd wager," Apedemak says as he wades toward Rah, tugging Gilgamesh along. "Help me with him."

Rah grabs onto Gilgamesh and smiles at his breathing but unusually silent body. Behind him, Amesemi wraps her arms around Apedemak. They lock eyes and, for once, she has no problem allowing him inside her mind.

Thank you...

Rah lets it linger for about as long as he can muster, then says, "We must get going. We're not yet safely home."

Amesemi opens her eyes and smiles at Apedemak. As he rubs the small of her back, she surveys the scene around her. She spots Nun's onyx slab a short distance away. "Actually, I think we are."

Apedemak and Rah's eyes follow Amesemi's extended finger toward Nun, who stands sentry upon his onyx disc. He nods toward them as they gather around their fallen comrade.

Then, kicking smoothly, they begin to bear Gilgamesh's unconscious form across the lake toward Nun's ship in the distance.

***

To Conquer a Demon—Rah's Personal Journal

We saved Gilgamesh, though his wounds require urgent attention.
What was that thing he awoke? A demon out of our darkest
nightmares; implacable, unstoppable…No; if I allow myself to
think like that, we all are lost. It can be stopped, if we work
together—if we have enough power…Somehow, I must get us that
power.

Will Nun offer any assistance, or does the old man truly
believe that we can overcome such a creature? Either way, there is
a new, disquieting sense of urgency, and time is not on our side.

***

It's dusk by the time the party spots the shore on the western
side of the Rift. They've traveled the entire distance in
complete silence, each of them trying to take in all that
they've just endured.

Gilgamesh coughs and splutters as he regains
consciousness. Nun stands, watching over him, his cloak
rippling in the breeze. For the entire journey, he has not let
his gaze leave Gilgamesh.

"What happened?" Nun asks, finally breaking his silence,
his concern apparent in his voice.

Apedemak stares at Nun, unable to conceal his
frustration. "We should be asking you—"

"Enough," Rah says, stepping before him and locking
eyes.

Apedemak's face grows dark, and his muscles tense, but

having little options, he swallows his anger and slowly nods.

Rah motions to Gilgamesh, who struggles into a sitting position. "You saw more than any of us. Tell him."

"Some rock monster," Gilgamesh says faintly. "It was three times as tall as me and had an open chest full of demonic fire…"

Amesemi looks to Nun with pleading eyes. "Do you know what it was?"

"Not what, but who. Coeus," Nun replies gravely.

Apedemak can no longer silence his fury. "These beasts have names now!" he erupts.

"He was more than a beast once," Nun rumbles. "Foremost among the Titans, perhaps the greatest of their number. He cared for humanity like no other. I created his race, and yet he might even have surpassed my ability as a watcher, given time."

They all stare agog at Nun's admission.

How could anyone, anything, surpass Nun's skill?

"But that thing showed no sign it was ever rational," Apedemak says.

"His curiosity was his undoing. He sought to reclaim the old relics—artifacts from the wreckage of the Sirius vessel—though I warned him to stay away," Nun says. "When he made contact with one of them…it destroyed his mind. His insatiable thirst for knowledge is now a hunger for souls at any cost."

Rah grimaces. "And you set this thing free?"

"I did. And there are many more. Countless other monstrosities wait for you beyond the Rift."

He takes in the stunned expressions on each of his progeny. "Now can you sense the depths of your naiveté?" He scoffs at their incredulous looks. "You honestly believed a few years of squabbling among yourselves meant you were ready to do battle with beings who had achieved godhood millennia before you were even born?"

There is a moment where all is silent save for the whisper of wind through the trees.

Rah is the first to speak, his voice full of humility. "So what would you have us do?"

The old man laughs, not unkindly. "Ah, my boy. The decisions are down to you from now on, remember? This is what you all wanted, this responsibility. Yet I can offer some advice."

They watch Nun expectantly. He gestures to Apedemak first. "You think yourself weak and resent Rah for the way his brute strength furthers his martial prowess. But there are subtleties to combat that he knows nothing of, which would stand you in good stead."

"Such as?" Apedemak asks, his head bowed in humility.

"There is a technique known as—a rough translation in your native tongue would be 'soul reinforcement,'" Nun says. "You can hone the weapons you carry with the energy of your psyche to literally will yourself to be a better warrior."

Gilgamesh, still regaining his strength, smirks slightly. "Seriously? If you give him the power to hate us to death, we won't last another day."

"The effect is only temporary," Nun says. "But make no mistake; I am not 'giving' anyone anything. This requires careful study. You —" He gestures to Amesemi. "You must immerse yourself in my libraries. Study this and all other information on the Ancients you can find. You think yourself smarter than the others? Prove it. Without knowledge of the secrets contained within the archives, Coeus and his kin will crush you."

Gilgamesh, rapidly healing, remains skeptical. "I could find all that out in mere minutes just by looking—"

"And fall down a hole again, no doubt," Apedemak says with a glare of vexation.

Gilgamesh visibly bristles. He grits his teeth, matching Apedemak's glare.

The vessel reaches the shore. An anxious Bydos comes running across the shoreline toward them, plainly bursting with questions. But upon his arrival, Rah silences him with a look.

"Is he so wrong?" Nun questions Gilgamesh. His aura turns a deep orange. He extends his finger close to Gilgamesh's face. "All too often you charge in without a moment's thought for the dangers that lie in wait. You could stand a better appreciation of caution—of how to be a tactician rather than a mere charlatan. As it stands, you are a wild card; unusable until you mature, you shall continue to fail and will inevitably fall to the first enemy who proves to be both as cunning and resourceful as you…and there are many who await such a challenge."

Bydos raises a curious hand. "And me?"

"Assist the others," Nun says. "Learn from your elders—"

"So that they may continue to treat me as a child?"

"Oh, you're not?" Gilgamesh asks with a smirk. "Did I miss something?"

"No need to be cruel," Apedemak objects.

"He speaks the truth, however unkind," Nun says. "You! *Child.* Would you challenge Coeus alone, then?"

"Coeus?" Bydos asks curiously.

Gilgamesh strains to sit up and shrugs his shoulder. "Oh you know, just the rock monster that Nun created who now surpasses even his power and almost killed us all."

Bydos scowls but shakes his head.

Nun nods. "Of course not. You are too small, too weak, and yet—"

"At least he knows that," Apedemak says, looking at Gilgamesh.

"And *yet*," Nun continues, "with that acceptance, he shows that someday perhaps he *will* face down a Titan."

Bydos smiles, pondering on this thought.

"No words of wisdom for me?" Rah asks.

"You're the leader," Apedemak says, shrugging in admission.

"Just so," Nun says to Apedemak. He sweeps his eyes and casts them upon Rah. "Be a leader. Heed my advice to the others. Follow their lessons, note their strengths and weaknesses, and show that you can command out of wisdom rather than fear."

Gilgamesh smiles, raising a finger. "Easier said than done."

Nun grunts. "Very true. This responsibility is, in itself, a test of sorts, possibly the hardest of them all…but I have said quite enough."

He looks up. The sky is dark now, the constellations visible in the black velvet above. "I must depart now. It's best I start fortifying the defenses around my own quarters as soon as possible. You all have six months until you leave this place. While it may seem like an age, it is anything but. Prepare yourselves well. You must accomplish much growth within this time frame if you are to succeed—if you are to survive."

With that, they hobble off Nun's ship, happy to be back on familiar ground. By the time they look back, Nun has already begun to propel the great onyx disc across the lake.

Rah salutes Nun in a slight gesture of thanks. In response, Nun raises a massive arm. Standing together on the shore, they watch as Nun's vessel recedes into nothingness upon the waters of the great lake.

They stand in silence, each pondering their respective missions while making failed attempts to envision just what the future holds for them. If the preceding two days are any indication, then the months to come will test their mettle to the core.

ABOUT THE AUTHOR

Manuel Godoy is the author of the popular comic series Kids 2 Kings and creator of the Black Sands universe. He is a military veteran, husband, and father of two loving children. He can be seen touring the Southeast doing book fairs, conventions, and other things. In his spare time, he loves playing video games and doing outside activities with his family.

PHNX (pronounced "Phoenix") is a musician, former radio host, stand-up comic, screenwriter, and actor. His passion for writing is second only to his belief that he is an immortal extraterrestrial, though his eight-year-old son and common colds tend to prove otherwise. He lives in Southern California with his wife, his son, a chameleon, and two wild birds, and he can usually be found wearing too much jewelry.